CW00822497

HOLLOW
OAK
PRESS

THROUGH THE BRIAR PATCH

Edited by

AMANDA PICA

For information about this title or to order addition print copies, please contact:
Hollow Oak Press
www.hollowoakpress.com

Cover design by Amanda Pica
Interior design by A.M. Gray

ISBN 979-8-9890118-2-7 (paperback)

Our puzzled hearts languish and linger on the platform until they catch the train of realization and ride it to the solution.

-Jebediah T. Atbash, Esquire

To The Puzzler Within:

Some may only read the stories, and that will always be enough.

But for those left:

For all the mysteries we've uncovered,

And felt perplexed enough to dig deeper.

For all the games we've won or lost,

Enter this one with a mind tenacious enough to see it through.

For all the joy we've found in curiosity,

The solution awaits.

Table of Contents

Ello, Gentle-reader, and welcome to our puzzle anthology, *Through the Briar Patch*. Within these pages, you'll find stories to surprise you, stories to make you think, and stories to entertain you. This book is not only to read, however. This book is also to decipher. Hidden within these pages are pieces and parts of puzzles to assemble into one final solution that will unlock a special feature.

That's right, we here at Hollow Oak enjoy plot twists so much, we made the entire book into one.

Everything you will need to produce the book's solution is contained in the physical copy you're holding right now. You will, however, need internet access to retrieve your special feature, should you solve the book. You may also choose to use the internet to help you solve some of the puzzles, and while there is no shame in using it as a tool, it's not a necessary one should you choose to go it alone.

In the case that you get stuck and aren't sure how to proceed, there are hints on our website, www.hollowoakpress.com, to use as another tool of assistance. The hints progress in the amount of information you're given, from broad nudges to more obvious clues. They are obscured by a simple cipher to prevent you from accidentally seeing a clue when you didn't want another one.

We've included a list of cipher names at the back of the book, as well. Not every cipher in the list is used among our pages, but we thought it prudent to include for anyone unfamiliar with the names of cipher types. For example, the Caesar cipher is a simple substitution cipher where each letter in the message is represented by a letter further down the alphabet, some fixed number of positions away from the original letter. This is the cipher we've used to encode the hints, and every hint is encoded with letters one position away from the original.

So, if we gave you the coded message HPPE MVDL, you would count one letter backward in the alphabet and substitute for the solution*. H would be G, P would O, etc.

As you complete the puzzles, you'll find a place to put your solutions in the back of the book. You'll find that the way you order your solutions will matter, and the key to their order can also be found if you know where to look.

As the late Jebediah T. Atbash once said, "Treachery is the tool of the damned." Unless, of course, that treachery is the kind we're giving you. Our kind is more delicious than a decadent chocolate torte: sought after and enjoyed, rich in its layers, and satisfying in its conclusion. If that damns us, then so be it.

You hold in your hands a book of such treachery. Each story will pull you into a world of deception, both within the story and within the pages itself. Tangle yourself up in our unreliable narrators, feast on our red herrings, and follow each page into the darkness ahead. We begin with a chilling story of how far we'll go to protect what we love.

Trust nothing. Believe no one. And keep a sharp eye out.

Yours in quixotic fun,
Amanda

* The solution to the sample Caesar cipher is GOOD LUCK

THE TREACHERY OF THE HEART

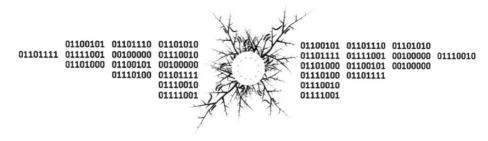

```
        01100101 01101110 01101010                              01100101 01101110 01101010
01101111 01111001 00100000 01110010                             01101111 01111001 00100000 01110010
        01101000 01100101 00100000                              01101000 01100101 00100000
                 01110100 01101111                              01110100 01101111
                          01110010                              01110010
                          01111001                              01111001
```

BY TIM JEFFREYS

Though the house she and Samuel occupied stood on a high crag, isolated and reached only by a narrow road, a road often blocked by snowfall in wintertime, Maggie sensed that it was a time to be vigilant. Every day, she left the house and walked the same circuit through the hills. Her route looked down, at all points, on the village—Dobcroft—which sat in the basin of the valley. Some days, seeing her donning coat and pulling on boots, Samuel stared at her like she was mad. "You're not going out there, are you, dear?" he'd say. "The rain's coming down at an angle."

That morning he'd risen before her and gone to his study. As she readied herself to leave the house, she'd called to him.

"I'm going for my walk."

She'd heard the study door open before she reached the front door. And he'd come rushing after her with hat, gloves, and scarf, his expression showing only concern. He'd thrust the things at her, saying, "Here. If you must go wandering about, take these. Looks like snow."

Setting out, she'd thought how it was in his little concerns for her that Samuel showed his love. She thought too that he may have been right; it was cold enough for snow, certainly. The sky had a dark, laden look to it. She wrapped the scarf around the lower half of her face and pulled the hat low on her brow. She wondered if Samuel would decide to take the car down to the village. Probably, he'd want to stock up in case it did snow and the road became impassable. It made her uneasy, thinking he might get stranded, leaving her alone at the house. He went to Dobcroft once or twice a week if the roads were open. She used to go with him, but she hadn't been to the village in weeks. Not since the time they'd gone and found the supermarket closed, with police tape cordoning off the pavement outside. Someone had told them it was because there'd been a shooting. Samuel had laughed at this. "A shooting? Here?" But she'd had an odd feeling, a feeling of being exposed, as if she'd turned around to find someone shining a very bright light into her face. The next time Samuel went to the village, he returned telling her he'd seen police officers going door to door.

"Something's going on down there," he'd said.

So she walked the same route every day, uncertain of what she was looking for, knowing only that she had to be watchful. And if when she returned to the house the telephone rang she let Samuel answer it; and at night, before going to bed, she double-checked the locks on the doors and windows. Lying awake, she made little plans in her head of where she'd go, and what she'd take with her if she had to leave the house in a hurry. And one time, left alone in the house, she'd gone to the hallway cupboard where Samuel kept the shotgun he used for clay pigeon shooting. There was a box of cartridges on a shelf. She'd held the gun in her hands, examining it until she thought she understood how it worked then she'd practised loading the cartridges.

It was on her return home that the sky began to spit snow. Samuel had been right, too, about her needing the hat, gloves, and scarf. She'd underestimated the cold. She pulled up the scarf so that only her eyes were exposed. If Samuel had gone to the village, she hoped he'd got the fire going before he left. She wanted to be in an armchair in front of it already, with a mug of hot tea, watching the snow drift past the window. She started to hurry.

She was within sight of the house when she noticed the young woman—or was it only a girl?—climbing the slope to her right; pale-faced, hugging herself, wearing nothing but a thin dress, her hair flapping like an orange flag. Thinking of Samuel, Maggie ducked down and started to run. But it was too late. The woman had lifted her head and spied her. Maggie straightened up, cursing herself for not bringing the shotgun with her on these walks. But Samuel, of course, wouldn't have allowed that. He'd have wanted to know why. Would've thought her crazier still.

For a few seconds both women froze, facing each other. Maggie, positioned on the crest of the hill, realised then that she had the advantage. She could run now, before the other woman had time to scramble up the remainder of the slope. She could get inside the house, draw the curtains, and lock all the doors. But she hesitated too long, and the orange-haired woman moved quick, rapidly closing the gap between them. Maggie's throat tightened. Pretending not to notice that the woman's feet were bare, she nodded and said, "Uh. Hello."

The other woman didn't answer. Snowflakes patterned her thick, orange hair. Her cheeks and nose were flushed with cold. Seeing her up close, Maggie thought she'd been right in thinking her only a girl. She was so slim and slight, a slip of nothing really. But there was something calculating in her gaze, something predatory. She walked in a slow circle around Maggie, looking her up and down. Then she halted, blocking the route back to the house, and her eyes narrowed and fixed on Maggie's.

"Cold," she said, hugging herself tighter and shivering as if to demonstrate. Her teeth chattered.

"Yes it is," Maggie said, deliberately misunderstanding. "Haven't you got a coat?"

"No time," the woman said. "Had to run."

Maggie looked towards Dobcroft. *Policemen going door to door,* Samuel had said, the last time he returned from the village. *Christ knows what they're looking for.*

She faced the young woman again, careful not to let her gaze stray beyond her to the house.

Stalling for time, she said, "You'll catch your death out here."

"That where you live?" the woman said, jerking her head in the direction of the house.

"Yes." Maggie did her best to keep her voice casual. A snowflake caught on one of her eyelashes, blurring her vision. She blinked it away. "Me and my husband."

"Husband?" The woman smirked. Turning, she looked at the house. Following her gaze, Maggie saw smoke pluming from the chimney. So Samuel had lit the fire. But was he still home? Or had he gone to Dobcroft? From where she stood, she couldn't see if the Land Rover was parked on the gravel patch alongside the house.

The woman returned her gaze to Maggie. "Looks lovely," she said. "Nice and cosy. And safe. How long?"

"I'm sorry."

"How long have you lived there?"

"Since...since I...since we got married."

The woman's smirk turned into a mocking smile. She leant forward. "And when was that, my love?"

Maggie took a step backwards. "I don't see that it's any of your..."

The woman startled her by making a quick grab at her scarf, trying to pull it away from her face. Pushing her hands away, Maggie staggered backwards, righting the scarf, ensuring that all but her eyes were covered. The woman lunged at her again, snatching the hat from her head and pulling at the scarf. With a wild cry, Maggie caught hold of the woman's arms. They struggled for a moment. Maggie felt the other's strength, pressing against her, the hands clawing at her. The pale, determined face, with blazing eyes and clenched teeth filled her vision. But then she found the strength to spin the woman around and throw her back down the slope. Without pausing, she frantically searched the ground for her hat, at the same time trying to cover her face again with the scarf. But one end had been yanked from inside her coat, and the wind toyed with it. She turned in circles, grasping at the loose end, blinded by the snow which was coming down harder, until she halted, hearing the other woman laughing.

She'd fallen only a short way down the slope before managing to check her tumble. She lay belly down in the grass, her arms crooked at her sides, hands braced against the ground as if at any moment she would spring to her feet. Her head was raised and she glared at Maggie, grinning.

Maggie covered her face with her gloved hands. Too late, though. Too late. She'd been seen. Reeling around in panic, she orientated herself in the direction of the house, and started to run. A ditch surprised her and she fell. Her chin struck the ground. Her teeth snapped together. Pain. Ice-cold water got inside her boot. Clambering to her feet, dazed, she ran on.

Not until she was meters from the house did she dare to look back. She swept her gaze one way, and then the other, searching through the fluttering snow for the orange-haired woman. Seeing no one, she let out her breath and laughed with relief. But the laughter died in her throat. Someone came over the crest of the low hill ahead of her.

Maggie gasped. "No."

Though dressed in the same clothes as the orange-haired woman, the approaching figure was not her. It was an older woman. Dark hair threaded with grey, sagging features. The thin white dress was tight on her, showing the folds of her body.

Dizzied by the pounding of her own heart, Maggie desperately searched her coat pockets for the house keys. Once inside, she closed the door and locked it. She went down the hall as quietly as she could, stopping outside the door to Samuel's study. Putting one ear to the door, she listened. Her ears were filled with the rushing of her own blood, but she heard nothing else. She would have to knock, or say his name, if she wanted to know for sure if he was inside. But she would not do that. Not yet. She crossed to the hallway cupboard where he kept his shotgun. Taking the gun down, she loaded the cartridges the way she'd practised. Turning back towards the front door, holding the gun in two hands, she heard the sound of a car engine outside.

"No," she said, shaking her head. "Samuel."

She ran to the lounge. The fire blazed in the hearth, and the room was warm. A wing-backed chair and footstool had been arranged close to the fire. Samuel must have moved them there, ready for her return. He really was the sweetest, kindest man she'd ever known. Looking up she saw, in the gilt-framed mirror above the hearth, the same face she'd seen on the figure outside: black hair threaded with grey, sagging features, big, frightened eyes. Crossing to the window, she looked out. She gasped. There was Samuel's Land Rover. And there was Samuel, standing beside it with his arm around… with his arm around that other…that…

When the two of them started towards the house, Maggie ducked away from the window. Not knowing what else to do, she rushed up the stairs. She stood on the landing, listening, as they entered the house.

Samuel's voice, incredulous: "What the hell were you thinking walking around outside dressed like that? Where did you even get that dress? And with nothing on your feet. Maggie…what on earth?"

Then, a perfect mimicry of her own voice, answering him: "I'm sorry, darling, I only popped out for a moment. I wanted to see the snow. I don't know what I was thinking."

Darling? That was a mistake. Maggie never called him 'darling.' Would he notice?

"Come in here," Samuel said, "and sit down by the fire."

Damn it. Maggie clenched one fist, thinking of that other woman sitting in the chair Samuel had set by the fireside. Set by the fireside for *her*. It was supposed to have been for her. She cradled the shotgun in both her hands, wondering what to do. Listening again, she heard Samuel's voice from below.

"I'll make you some tea."

Footsteps in the hall. When she heard him rattling cups in the kitchen, she crept back down the stairs and into the lounge. The other woman was in the wing-backed chair facing the fire with her bare feet up on the footstool. All Maggie saw was the crown of her head. Raising the shotgun, she crept forward into the room. She halted when the other woman, without turning around, spoke in a low tone.

"What are you going to do?" A soft chuckle. "Shoot me?"

Maggie realised she'd forgotten about the mirror above the hearth.

"Get out," Maggie hissed. "Get out, or…or I'll blow your head off."

The woman turned and peered around the chair-back. "And how will you explain that to him?"

"I'll tell him the truth," Maggie said.

"What?" The woman laughed under her breath again. "The whole truth?"

"I don't know what you mean."

The other woman shook her head. "How long have you been here, living like this? Long enough to forget?"

"Get out. This is *my* home."

The woman was silent for a few moments. "Sister," she said then in a low voice, "it's him we should get rid of. We can live here together, you and I."

"I…I'm not your sister."

"Who are you then? Do you think he knows? Do you think he's known all along?"

Hearing footsteps approaching the room, Maggie crabbed backwards and ducked behind the door. She held her breath, hearing Samuel enter the room.

"Here we are, dear," Samuel said. "Nice hot tea. This should do the trick."

The imposter's voice: "Thank you, darling. You are kind. Listen, I'm a little peckish now too. You couldn't make me a sandwich, could you? Please. Pretty please."

"Of course I could. What do you want on it?"

"Oh, anything. Just throw it all on there."

Wrong. Tuna mayonnaise. Maggie liked tuna mayonnaise.

"I'll see what there is."

When she heard Samuel retreating down the hall to the kitchen again, Maggie slid out from behind the door. But the other woman must have leapt to her feet the moment Samuel left the room, as she was suddenly there in Maggie's face, grabbing the barrel of the shotgun in two hands, trying to wrench it out of Maggie's hands. In silence, they struggled for possession of the gun.

"Give it to me, sister," the woman hissed into Maggie's face. "If you don't want to kill him, I'll do it. We can live here together, you and I. No one has to know. The village isn't safe for our kind anymore. I'll be him, and you keep the woman's face if that's what you want."

"I don't know what you're talking about," Maggie hissed back. "For the last time, I'm not your sister."

The woman gritted her teeth, pulling at the gun barrel. "Do you think I can't recognise my own kind? Do you think I can't smell it? Do you think I didn't know from the moment I put eyes on you?" Fury darkened the woman's face. She pulled hard on the gun, almost yanking it out of Maggie's hands.

"Give it to me! Do you want to go back to the dark, sister? Huh? Back to the cold? Back to that miserable hole in the ground? Give me the gun. It's him or you. I'm not going back there."

Without warning, she savagely head-butted Maggie in the face. Pain exploding around her nose, Maggie fell back with a muffled cry. The gun slipped out of her grasp. The other woman had it now. Seeing her swinging around towards the door with a look of triumph on her face, Maggie dived. She and the other woman crashed together to the floor, rolling, struggling, once again fighting for possession of the gun.

Samuel shouted from the kitchen. "There's some lettuce. Do you want lettuce, dear?"

Maggie and the other woman fell still.

"Yes!" they shouted in unison, before resuming their struggle.

Thinking of the way Samuel cared for her, his tenderness, Maggie found renewed determination, renewed strength. Pushing the other woman down against the floor, she fought to get astride her. Both still had hold of the gun, but Maggie put her weight on top of it, forcing the barrel across the other woman's throat.

"Please…" the woman said. "…sister…"

"I told you," Maggie said, pressing the shotgun barrel harder into the woman's neck. "I'm not your bloody sister."

The other woman's face contorted with a silent scream. Her tongue darted out of her mouth. Her eyes bulged. But she made no sound except for a thin rattle. Not until feeling the body beneath her go slack did Maggie stop pressing down. As soon as she did, she clamoured to her feet. Setting the shotgun down behind the door, she returned to the prone woman and, realising there was no time to check for a pulse, she hooked her hands into the woman's armpits and dragged her towards the door. Before leaving the lounge, she leant back and shouted, in as controlled a voice as she could muster, towards the kitchen.

"Toast the bread, will you, dear?"

"What?" Samuel shouted back.

"I said toast the bread for me, please!"

"*Toast* it?" Samuel's incredulous voice came back.

"Yes, I want it toasted."

"But I've already…"

"What, dear?"

"I've already…never mind. I'll start again."

Without hesitating, Maggie got her hands back under the woman's armpits and dragged her out of the lounge. The kitchen door was open at the end of the hall. If Samuel should emerge, if he should see her…

She pushed the thought from her mind. As silently as she could, she dragged the woman to the front door. Carefully, she drew back the bolts and got the front door open. The snow had turned to a blizzard. She could see nothing beyond a few feet in front of her. Dragging the woman out, she dumped her to one side of the door, pleased to think that the snow would quickly cover the body. Dead or alive, it didn't matter. She would deal with it later, perhaps that night when Samuel was asleep. Hurrying back inside, she eased the door shut and rushed to the lounge where she fell down into the wing-backed chair. The heat from the fire felt good. Kicking off her boots, she put her feet up on the footrest just as she heard Samuel's footsteps in the hall.

When he appeared with the sandwich, he stood over her with a bewildered look.

"My god, Maggie," he said. "Your nose is bleeding."

"Is it?" She touched a finger to her lip, saw blood on it. "So it is."

"Here," Samuel said, taking a handkerchief from his pocket and handing it to her. "Whatever happened?"

"Nothing." She dabbed at her nose with the handkerchief. "It's just one of those things."

He looked along her body. "And you got changed?"

"Of course!" Realising she sounded half-crazed, she took a deep breath to calm herself. "You didn't think I was going to sit around in a thin little dress all day, did you? On a day like this?"

"What I don't understand," Samuel said, in a reprimanding tone. "Is why you were wearing that thin little dress in the first place."

"I found it in the back of my wardrobe, that's all, and I was trying it on when I saw the snow coming down and I rushed outside to see it. I do love the snow. Don't look so bewildered, dear. I wasn't thinking, that's all."

It was a poor explanation, at which Samuel narrowed his eyes but he didn't question her further. She often wondered if he knew the truth. She'd been careful, and had spent some time watching his wife, the real Maggie Harris, studying her mannerisms and modes of speech before that day when she'd seen Samuel climb into his Land Rover and drive away, and she'd finally approached the house. She remembered how Maggie Harris' face had looked when she answered the door. Surprised, but amiable.

Can I help you?

She'd buried the body in a shallow grave far out on the moor, in a spot even she couldn't have found again, and had installed herself at the house before Samuel returned. She would do the same thing with the body outside if it was still there by nightfall. *Back to the dark, sister. Back to the cold.* She had a good thing here. It was cosy and safe, just like the woman had said when they faced each other out on the hillside. And she had a man who loved her. She wasn't going to make any foolish missteps like calling him 'darling.' Things that would make him suspicious. And if a knock should come on the front door, she would escape out the back. Who knows where she would go then, what face she would choose. She would be sad to leave Samuel, true. A man so doting was not easy to find.

Maggie watched the thick snowflakes cascading past the window. Judging by the way it was coming down out there, there'd be no knock on the door for a few weeks at least. Plenty of time to think. Plenty of time to make a plan.

He remained standing, looking quizzically at her. "Are you sure you're all right, dear?"

She looked at him, standing so tall over her. He remained a handsome man, despite his age, with a full head of hair, perfectly white. He was in his seventies now and so, she remembered, was she. Never once had he asked her why she didn't look a day over fifty-five.

And as for that miserable hole in the ground. Ha! That miserable hole in the ground was a long time ago. She'd lived here long enough to forget, yes, and indeed she almost had. She hardly thought about her beginnings anymore, or wondered where they were, the others. It was another life. But if ever there was a time to remember, it was a time like this, when she sat in front of the blazing fire, with her feet up on the stool and a mug of hot tea in her hand, watching snow fall past the window.

Turning to Samuel, she showed him a smile. The way he looked at her now, head cocked, brow knit, made her wonder if he did know, if he had known all along. Perhaps he preferred things this way. After all, she was nothing if not malleable. Unlike the real Maggie Harris, she could mould herself to suit his needs.

"Darling," she said, testing him, watching his face. She saw not a flicker. "Don't fret. I'm perfectly fine."

When we're young, the modern English alphabet serves as the building blocks for our developing language skills. We practice the sing-song list of letters in order, then move on to understanding their sounds and how they group together, and that leads us eventually to a mastery of the written language we use in almost every facet of daily life. This entire book you're holding in your hands is comprised of a set of twenty-six characters mixed and matched in ways that form meaning while you're looking at them.

Isn't language amazing?

People didn't always use a set of letters to represent sounds. Early written language consisted of pictographs that represented words, like the hieroglyphs of ancient Egypt or cuneiform in Mesopotamia. The first letters were invented by ancient Egyptians and consisted of a set of twenty-four glyphs called uniliterals that each represented a sound and were used to aid in pronunciation and grammatical structure for the other glyphs. Uniliterals evolved into the Proto-Sinaitic script, the earliest alphabetic script, which eventually developed into the Phoenician alphabet as early as 1050 BC. Phoenician merchants carried these letters to other cultures, and they were used to write several different languages, and served as the basis for other alphabetic systems. Over thousands of years, this first alphabet has become the letters you are using right now, to read this both this information and the stories scattered throughout this book.

THE EAST FRANKLIN PUZZLE

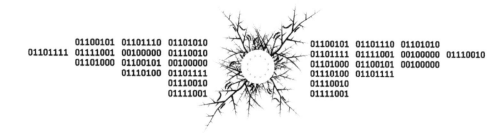

```
              01100101 01101110 01101010                    01100101 01101110 01101010
    01101111  01111001 00100000 01110010                    01101111 01111001 00100000 01110010
              01101000 01100101 00100000                    01101000 01100101 00100000
                       01110100 01101111                    01110100 01101111
                       01110010                             01110010
                       01111001                             01111001
```

BY R .C. CAPASSO

"It's hard to imagine the club without Nora." Delia wore a lace-trimmed black blouse and long skirt, with black shoes that came to uncomfortable-looking points at the toes. She hadn't donned mourning because she was so very close to the deceased, but funerals gave her an opportunity to dress up.

"I know. But I'm sure she'd want us to continue. Nora put so much of herself into all her organizations." Stephanie surveyed the plates of finger food arranged on the large round table. It had been a good decision to invite everyone back here after the graveside service.

They stood in the community room of the small East Franklin library. Every Thursday evening for years a group of committed jigsaw puzzlers had met to put together the latest challenge. Never anything short of a thousand pieces. The harder the better. And Leonora Allan Wilding, fondly known as Nora, had been the perpetual president of the Puzzlers Club, provider of lemon bars and gingersnaps for snack time, and frequent donor of the next high-quality puzzle. It seemed natural to gather in their meeting space after the funeral.

"You know, she never put in the last piece herself. She always let someone else do it." Maria Luisa, the high school principal, raised a glass of punch in a kind of salute.

Stephanie, the librarian, nodded. "I know. I used to watch her slide pieces toward someone so they could 'find' them and fill in a critical area. For someone in charge, she was always behind the scenes, never trying to get attention."

A short man in a dragging raincoat stumped into the room. "That's why we have to dedicate the next puzzle to her." Shoving aside a plate of brownies, he laid a square, flat package wrapped in brown paper onto the puzzle table.

"That's not a completed puzzle, is it, Doug?" The group was strict about the community nature of their projects; no one worked alone outside of the meetings, and no one brought in previously completed works. Of course, Doug had just joined recently, dropping in one night, silent and focused solely on the puzzle in progress. He wasn't a talker, so who knew if he really understood the aim of the group?

"Of course it's not completed." Doug's bushy eyebrows grew together in a scowl. He knew he was no one's favorite person, but he had an address in East Franklin and no one could bar him from coming to a library function. "It's a photo I took. Of Nora's place. Where she was happiest, once. I thought I'd have it made into a puzzle, and we could do it in her honor." Ignoring the surprised looks—was it so hard to believe that he might have a kindly thought?—he pulled off the paper and revealed a large photo of Nora's house and garden.

"Oh, the cottage," Delia sighed.

There was no other word for the small structure, with its bright green door, steeply pitched roof, windows open to let soft white curtains float with the breeze, and flowers everywhere, trailing up the walls on vines, lining the stone walkway and tumbling around the corners to disappear behind the cottage into a garden you could imagine pouring out into the woods behind. The setting sun behind the viewer cast reflected tones of pink and purple in the sky above the roof, and lights in each window sent a message of welcome.

"She loved that house," Stephanie confirmed.

"I'm thinking 2,000 pieces." Doug glanced at each of them quickly. "Make the project last."

Smiles and nods sealed the plan, and Doug gathered up the picture and its wrapping. All his effort had been worthwhile; the picture had finally turned out looking good.

"It's such a cute cottage. But I just saw it from the road, passing by. Was it as pretty inside?" Rita, mother of three, who attended every library children's event and allowed herself only this one night out as an adult, leaned forward with a piece that looked like part of a pink hydrangea bloom. She was always drawn to dreaming about other houses—not that she wasn't perfectly happy with her own split-level on a quarter acre lot.

There was a moment of silence as people exchanged glances around the circle.

"Well, I never actually went inside." Stephanie kept her voice carefully smooth; she was the librarian, a figure of some standing in the community, after all, so maybe Nora, always thoughtful and deferential, hadn't felt comfortable making the next step of inviting her over as a simple friend.

"Me neither." Two others spoke at the same time.

It turned out that no one had ever stepped foot in Nora's cottage.

"But she was so hospitable." Anthony frowned slightly. He was 27 and a local police officer who had joined the club as a way to do community outreach while at the same time forcing himself into some form of relaxation. "I mean, she was probably just super private. You know, more comfortable going out to people than having them in." He thought of his chaotic apartment and suddenly felt closer to the elderly lady.

"Oh, yes. Nora was the sweetest person." They all agreed.

"How long did she live there, anyway?" Anthony could still smell one house he'd entered, the one where he learned the meaning of "hoarding."

"Oh, forever." Delia laughed. "I mean, I was a kid and she was in that house. Pam, what do you think?"

Pam pursed her lips. As obviously the oldest member of the club, except for the now deceased Nora, she was supposed to know everything about the town. As if she were a gossip. "I could not tell you. I moved here when I married 45 years ago, and Nora was in the cottage then. By herself. Older than me. And don't ask about her family, because I have no idea."

"Hmmm." Stephanie wasn't feeling so much an outsider anymore. "Well, in any case Nora must have been very attached to the place. And she couldn't have been more engaged in our community. We'll all have to produce double our usual goodies for the museum's bake sale to make up for her contributions." She scanned the original photo of Nora's cottage. "Does anyone see where a sort of dark shape should go?" She held up a puzzle piece. "It's got two knobs and this curve at the bottom."

"I'd say here." Carl, a divorced dentist, tapped his finger. "In the left bottom window."

Stephanie stared at the picture, slid the piece into place, and turned the picture toward the group. "Yes, the piece fits. But the photo shows a light there, a lamp. Not a dark spot in the window."

"Dang it." Doug leaned forward. "I took care of that."

No one said a word as Doug pushed back from the table, grabbed his coat off the rack, and stomped out. Anthony just checked his watch, the way he did every time car tires squealed, voices raised, or his downstairs neighbor slammed the street door. You never know what you are witnessing.

Stephanie stood off to the side, sipping her decaf. In a minute she'd go wash her hands, so that no trace of the peanut butter cookies from the group snack would transfer to the puzzle. So far she hadn't said anything, because she must be mistaken. That piece she'd placed in the window the week before, the dark shape, now looked like a lamp and part of the curtain. Just as the picture indicated. So had she imagined that conversation and Doug stamping off?

No one had access to the puzzle during the week. It slid on a board into the storage closet at the far corner of the room. A locked closet that held donations to the library, reams of paper, decorations for kids' programming, and an old tape recorder. No one could have entered and substituted a puzzle piece or altered the piece itself with paint or markers. The surface was smooth, just as it would have come from the puzzle maker.

The change in the image wasn't worth mentioning, and yet...she felt just the slightest bit odd.

The group was unusually quiet that evening, with several people glancing at the puzzle, then the picture, and then down to their little pile of pieces. Doug came in late, looked at the cottage as it was growing steadily in its garden, frowned and then shook himself.

"Um, excuse me." Delia placed a couple pieces next to the left side of the cottage, near a large lilac shrub. "Can someone check these pieces, because I think they fit but they shouldn't?" Her soft voice rose about an octave.

Carl leaned forward. "No, you're good."

"Yeah, but..." Maria Luisa stood and walked over to Doug's photo propped on an easel just behind Stephanie. "They look like, what, a person? Kind of shadowy. But there's nobody in the photo."

Doug let out a brief word totally out of keeping with the tone of the club meetings.

Stephanie, nominally in charge since it was her building, made herself push her chair back and step over to pick up the enlarged photo, bringing it to the table.

"Yeah, I don't see..." Delia bit her lip. "That's why I thought I was mixed up."

"And now there's a lamp in the window, where there was a shadow last week. Remember when we talked about that?" Anthony felt an urge to pull out a notebook and write this down. "Everyone sees that, right?"

Doug swore again, and Stephanie couldn't make herself reprimand him.

He jumped up, grabbed his coat, and shoved a hand into one sagging pocket. Anthony flung out an arm, as if to gesture everyone to move behind him. And damn it, he was unarmed.

But it was paper, glossy paper, Doug pulled out of the pocket and slapped onto the table, sending a pile of sky pieces skittering across the board.

"It's in every one, and it keeps moving."

Carl reached for a photo, studied it, then passed it to Delia. One by one, the snapshots made the round of the table, counterclockwise. Anthony held each by the edges, as if to preserve any fingerprints, although he was the fifth person to handle them.

Doug jabbed a stubby finger at the photos, now spread over the incomplete puzzle. "I went out on a clear evening. I wanted the sunset color and softness on the flowers. I know what I'm doing with photography. But when I went over the shots, to select the best one, I kept seeing this blasted shadow."

He pointed to the marred photos, now spread across the incomplete puzzle. "In the window. Beside the house. On the path. In an upstairs window. And one..." He pulled a final photo from his coat. "One in my face."

The image showed a dark smudge across most of the photo's surface, with just bits of the house and woods and sky around the edges.

Pam frowned. "Why aren't any of the shadows in the picture you used for the puzzle?"

"I edited them out." Doug's voice was raw. "And it wasn't easy. Every time I removed one, another blotch appeared somewhere else. It took hours to get an image that was clear."

Pam met his eyes. "And yet the puzzle's not clear now. The dark spot keeps coming back. Here and there. Nothing permanent. Moving from one piece to another."

Delia took a step back. Stephanie rubbed her arms.

"Why is the room so cold?" Carl eyed Doug's stained coat with something like desire.

"We have to go to Nora's house." Anthony's voice was high but firm. "Carl, Doug, you're with me. Ladies, please make your way home and wait to hear from us."

"Oh, no way." Pam, who always had a sweater, pulled it around her. "I can take three in my car."

The house looked remarkably like it did in the growing puzzle. Rose and purple streaks from the sunset at their backs cast fainter, cooler shades into the sky behind the house. Some of the flowers had faded, their heads dipping down toward the ground, but new ones were opening for the later season. Someone must have been taking care of the property; it still looked lived in.

Especially with a shadow in the right window. A shadow that faced them, as they lined up at the edge of the stone walkway. As they halted, motionless, the dark shape slowly, deliberately moved aside revealing crisp white curtains.

"You're sure she had no family?" Delia's voice trembled.

"No one." Pam stared straight ahead. "Doug, you came onto the property and took photos. You're the closest thing we have to a stalker. Did you see anyone?"

"No. The shadows appeared when I looked at the pictures on my computer." He glared at the building. "They didn't reveal themselves to my naked eyes."

"Then something's changed. Because I see a dark shape." Stephanie swallowed. "Something is asking us in."

"It better be Nora." Anthony ached to pull his weapon from its holster, click it, and grip it in his hands. But he had nothing. Just a sense of cold that was turning his insides frigid. "On my count. One..."

But Doug was already moving, with Pam one step behind. They went straight to the house, and Doug grabbed the doorknob.

"It's probably..." Anthony could not get the words out before the door swung open with a teeth-chattering creak.

They all made their way in, stumbling on feet as cold as if they'd been standing on ice. The front door opened into a small living room, barely able to hold them all, but they didn't mind standing close together. They never got a glance at the furnishings, because their eyes were all drawn to the back wall.

A shadow loomed from the floor up to the ceiling. But no matter how they twisted their heads to look for light, they knew that the shade was not formed by any of them.

"It's freezing," Carl muttered.

"I'm sorry."

They jumped and grabbed each other as Nora's voice came faintly, but clearly. "I wish I could send it away."

"Nora?" Pam whispered the name. She was the one who'd known her longest, after all. Though she really hadn't known her at all.

"It's always been here with me. I could fight it better when I was younger. I had some skills, some gifts." The voice sounded like it was coming through the walls. "But now that I'm…" Even her ghost seemed to recoil before the word "dead." "I used to be able to escape for a little. I came out every chance I could get, hiding among you all. You were so kind…But now it's—" The voice stopped with a kind of gasp.

"Nora?" Stephanie forced her voice to be firm, like she was calling the children's story group to order.

It seemed as if the walls themselves sighed. "Please. Help."

"What can we do?" Delia stared at the others. "Get a priest or something?"

"No use in that." Doug gave a vague dismissive wave of his hand.

Pam faced him. "How do you know?"

"It's a waste of time."

No one dared ask why.

Stephanie took a step forward. "Nora, tell us what to do."

But a great wave of cold passed over them, shuddering down their spines, stinging their eyes into tears.

As he swiped his eyes clear with a shaking hand, Anthony spoke. "Out. Everybody. We regroup outside."

The evening air warmed them slightly even as the sunlight faded.

"No wonder she never let anyone in." Pam stared back at the house. "Can you imagine going in, just one of us? Alone?"

"So what do we do?" Anthony looked from Doug to Stephanie.

"What can we do?" The librarian still clasped her arms around her chest, trying to still her trembling. "There's no way to deal with something that can't even be real."

"Oh, it's real," Delia whispered. "But we're just people. We've got nothing."

"We have a puzzle." Doug planted himself before them.

"But..." Carl began.

"He's right." Stephanie unclasped her arms to point a shaking finger at Doug. "That thing tried to hold Nora, but she escaped to us. She snatched little pieces of life from us, to keep going. We mean something to her. The town means something. We've got to pull her out."

Anthony straightened. "We've got to claim her."

Doug turned, heading back to the parked cars. "Tell your friends. Tomorrow, all day. At the puzzle."

Word about a commemorative project for Nora spread through conversations at the post office, the convenience store, the little bakery on South Street. By the time Stephanie unlocked the doors at 10:00, people clustered on the sidewalk. Several had brought snapshots of Nora, because one proposal was to make a collage to hang in the community room.

Volunteers moved through the puzzle room all day. Some could only stay long enough to put two pieces together, then leave it to someone else to fit them in place. A couple scrapbookers made the collage, pasting in Nora's recipes and newspaper clippings next to the photographs.

"She never aged, did she?" someone commented, looking at a photo from 1982.

"She never got young, either," Doug growled.

Stephanie studied the photos. It was true. Delia had brought in a picture from 1990 showing her younger self, thinner and with neat cornrows, receiving a high school award from Nora, president of the scholarship committee. Nora wore a dress Stephanie recognized from the last library spring fair. Next to this photo lay a faded, curling picture of Nora from a newspaper account of the town sesquicentennial in 1958. She looked exactly as Stephanie knew her. Feeling Doug's eyes on her, she turned, but he was already at the other side of the room.

Newcomers asked why there were dark pieces that seemed to fit a space but not match the enlarged photo serving as their guide. Pam said there had been a problem with the company that turned the photo into a puzzle.

Maria Luisa suggested there might have been water damage in the mail.

Carl blamed the glare from the overhead lights, which made glossy pieces hard to match easily.

As for the cold in the room, which kept intensifying, Stephanie claimed she'd called for repairs. By 2:00 the village volunteers had slipped away. They didn't understand why large areas of the puzzle were now dark, like it was supposed to be a picture of a cave or storm clouds at night.

Stephanie posted an announcement on the website about a power outage and sent the rest of the small staff home.

"Are we making things worse?" Delia stood back. Whenever she didn't have to pick up a puzzle piece, she thrust her hands into mittens.

"It's not happy." Pam swallowed. "That thing. So, is it good that it's not happy?"

"There's one way to find out." Doug pushed a piece with the tip of his finger. "Seven more pieces. One for each of us."

Carl took a step back. "Um..."

"Oh, come on." Anthony grabbed a dusky piece with three knobs. "Man up."

"Or woman." Pam followed him, then gestured to Delia.

The lights flickered. The door to the main room of the library slammed.

When two pieces remained, Stephanie could see her breath. "You or me?"

Doug narrowed his eyes. "I'll do the last one."

Stephanie's hands shook so that she dropped the penultimate piece. Diving under the table, she scraped at the floor to pull it into her palm. As her head hit the edge of the table coming up, she could have sworn she heard a laugh, low, guttural and mean. But she didn't even look to see if the others had reacted. She stood, dropped the piece onto the puzzle and pushed it slowly, rotating it until it slid reluctantly into place.

The four pieces around it buckled, popping up, but Anthony brought his palm down and smashed them flat.

Without speaking, everyone edged toward the exit as Doug put in the final black piece.

The puzzle burst into flames.

Stephanie grabbed Delia and Carl while Anthony reached for the fire extinguisher and, for the first time since his training, used it.

It was late afternoon before they finished giving statements to the fire department and the police officer, who stared long and hard at Anthony.

When the library parking lot was finally cleared, they piled into two cars and drove to Nora's place.

The sunset was the best yet; they'd missed a gorgeous fall day and hadn't noticed, caught within the library walls for hours.

They stood in a line again, facing the silent house.

Stephanie took a step forward and halted, feeling something under her soft, thin work shoes.

She bent and picked up two small puzzle pieces, linked together.

They formed the figure of a small woman, smiling, sun on her face.

Nora.

"The door's open." Delia looked up from the pieces and pointed to the house.

They edged in, then spread throughout the first floor. A little dust lay on the furniture, but a scent of flowers came through the open windows. The temperature was still warm from the afternoon sun.

"It's okay, isn't it?" Stephanie instinctively turned to find Doug.

But he wasn't there. Not in the house, not on the property, not in Anthony's car.

Not in town, ever again.

But he'd done his bit.

Early glyphs to illuminated manuscripts to Tumblr, language has evolved as long as humans have been on the earth. Language plays a central role in how we interact with each other. We've striven to understand each evolving sentence structure, bit of grammar, and word usage as they've shifted and grown with our communication needs.

We can traverse history back as far as the stone age to compare how language has changed, but we don't need to. We can stay in the modern era, because language is evolving right before our eyes.

Every generation has had slang terms that become part of a common vernacular, and every previous generation has had people who sneer at the way "kids these days" talk. As forms of written communication with a broad reach have become more accessible, the evolution of written language has become part of this larger conversation. Gone are the days when widely-seen written language was relegated to books, magazines, and newspapers.

With the rise of social media, blogging, and group chats, people are communicating with written language on a much wider scale than in previous generations, and language and grammar have evolved specific to those platforms. Rapidly shifting terminology has increased with the ease of transmission the internet provides.

On a blog, you're more likely to see a range of styles, from somewhat more informational to a more personal, story-telling feel. Blogs tend to use rule-based grammar and punctuation, though with a slightly less formal tone.

In the early days of texting, shortened words became the norm, likely because the number of keystrokes on cell phones at the time made texting cumbersome. Abbreviations, acronyms, and symbolic language, such as swapping letters and numbers, became widespread. Some are still used.

Currently in a text, a period at the end of a message indicates a tonal shift from neutral conversation to a curt abruptness that may indicate irritation or annoyance. Emojis brought another era of tone to text-based communication. These are a playful way to indicate intent by inserting a picture-based indication of mood into the text.

Where language goes from here is anyone's guess. The one constant is that everything changes, and while we may not be able to predict the content of those changes, we can be sure that our language will remain as malleable and ever-shifting as it was in prehistoric times.

Cold Food

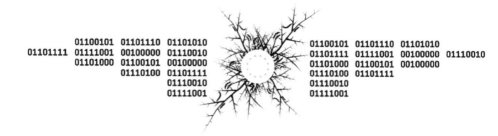

01100101 01101110 01101010
01101111 01111001 00100000 01110010
01101000 01100101 00100000
01110100 01101111
01110010
01111001

01100101 01101110 01101010
01101111 01111001 00100000 01110010
01101000 01100101 00100000
01110100 01101111
01110010
01111001

by A. M. Gray

It was 8:15 p.m. on an icy east coast Friday when Morgan decided her husband was having an affair.

She decided this, not with anger or malice, but with the sanitized precision of someone who was tired of eating cold food.

"Sorry I'm late sweetheart," David called from downstairs, the sound of the door closing behind him echoing up to her like a judge's gavel.

"What kept you so long?"

"Stayed late for work again, it's been one hell of a busy quarter."

Work again? Morgan seriously doubted that.

She got out of their bed, not bothering with the sheets that fell to the floor behind her, and made her way downstairs to welcome home the man she hoped she could still love.

His cropped blonde hair was wet from the slushy mix falling outside, his fine suit dotted with ice and road salt. David's blue eyes were too small for his nose and his chin was weak, marked with a scar from a bar fight, or at least so he claimed.

His eyes didn't widen when they saw her, pupils didn't dilate with primal need, he may as well have seen her in sweatpants as opposed to the bright red lingerie she'd gotten herself for her birthday.

"You look good, Morgs," he said lamely, like a teenager who was pretending to be interested in economics class.

She wanted to tell him to get the fuck out of their house, that she knew what he was doing.

"Thank you," she said instead, turning and walking into the kitchen where their now cold Chinese was sitting in its brown paper bags on their tiny hand-me-down table.

They sat, Morgan resisting the urge to shiver from the cold, and began to dig into their meals. The 3-hour-old takeout tasted like ash in her dry mouth. She looked across the table to see David's response and stopped chewing mid-mouthful.

David's eyes were closed, his lips moving in a mumbled prayer as he grasped some necklace under his shirt.

The new girl must be religious.

Morgan couldn't make sense of the words he was saying, only that him praying at all was *wrong.*

"You saying something?" she asked.

His eyes opened, shoulders tensing as he stared at the table in front of her, his ears turning red as his knuckles whitened their grip on the necklace.

"Nothing for you to worry about," he said forcefully, all but growling as he pulled his hand away from his shirt and moved it to his food.

Since when did he have the fucking nerve to talk to her like that?

They ate in a silent uncompanionship, dissecting their food like the fermented frogs she remembered from freshman year biology class.

"So, uh… how was your day Morgs?" He didn't look at her.

"Fine I guess, went to work, came home, waited for you. The usual."

"Gotcha…"

"What about you, anything fun?"

"Not really, just lots of—" his phone buzzed, making the fork he had been using to eat lo mein clatter against the table. Two buzzes, a text message.

He had stopped mid-sentence, but he resisted the urge to check the phone, refusing to meet Morgan's eyes as he picked the fork back up and continued to poke at his noodles.

"Work stuff?" she asked, daring him to open the message.

"Probably… I'll get it later."

They finished up in about fifteen minutes, Morgan put their silverware in the sink before tossing out the plastic food containers in their stainless-steel trash can. Her thigh brushed the cold metal, and she felt goosebumps rise up across her body.

When she turned around, David had already gone into the living room, leaving his chair pulled out and a dirty napkin on the table.

As well as his phone.

Morgan's hands started shaking, sudden doubt flooding through her, thoughts of misunderstandings and the importance of trust.

She threw those thoughts through a brick wall.

The phone's sleek case was still faintly warm from being in David's pocket, the crack in the center of the screen smiling up at her. Her thumb found the power and she was greeted with his two-and-a-half-year-old wallpaper of them at the Grand Canyon. She remembered the smell of dust whipping about them as they held each other, close to the ledge, smiling in the sunset. She had been a stick back then, before his distance had driven her back to the gym for a distraction.

Under the time—which he had in military as a throwback to their ROTC days—was a solitary message notification.

V: thanks for the meal, same time next week right?

Morgan's shaking hands solidified, hardened like her heart was under the red lace she had put on for him. She swiped her thumb up and put in the password, each number giving a faint rumble that felt like an earthquake running through her.

Incorrect password

She tried two more times before she heard the floorboards creak in the hall.

"*Shit!*" she whispered under her breath as she placed the phone on the table and rushed to the sink to pretend she was washing their forks. He came in behind her, and Morgan held her breath as she waited for him to see the wrong password notifications.

He opened a cupboard instead, the crinkle of the potato chip bag sounding for the first time in her life like a relief instead of a crumby annoyance.

"I'm gontha h'ad up 'ta bed," he said to her back through a mouthful of chips.

He took his phone with him.

Morgan didn't miss the opportunity, having already ripped the Band-Aid of blissful ignorance off, she set around the downstairs. She checked his coat pockets, his cluttered car in the garage, the end table next to his spot on the couch. She even checked between the fucking couch cushions. As she lifted the first one she thought she was losing her mind, but when she found the shiny bronze key under the third cushion, she half wished she hadn't looked.

The key was old, not one of the ones you could get cloned at those loud machines at the hardware store. This key had knobs at the handle end and was covered in intricate scrollwork all along its length.

V must have money to live in a place with doors like that.

Morgan pulled out her phone, snapping a picture of it before she carefully set it under the couch for David to find later. She kept searching.

When it hit midnight and Morgan hadn't found anything else of substance, she resigned herself to bed. The thought of sleeping next to him made her feel physically ill, but she climbed the stairs anyway.

David's lamp was still on for her to see by, he was passed out on his side, the potato chip bag laying half empty on the floor beside the bed. On his nightstand, the book cover for *The Two Towers* looked somehow even looser and more disheveled on the beat-up hardback than it had the last time he'd read it a few months ago. She couldn't even remember him going through Fellowship this time, but he was a habitual re-reader, she had no doubt missed it. She used to track the days of the week by the progress of his bookmark, back when he'd read beside her on the couch while she watched the news. He just went upstairs these days.

Morgan threw the rest of the chips in the bathroom trashcan and stepped to the sink. Rivers of eyeshadow and tears washed down the drain. She tossed on a baggy T-shirt and a pair of basketball shorts to sleep in, hiding the self-conscious shame he made her feel under the layers of cotton.

The cool, coarse metal of the bar bit into Morgan's hands, her chest and shoulders screaming in pain.

Two more reps.

Her breath came out ragged as she moved the weight down to touch her chest, the fabric of the bench slick with sweat under her back.

Up again.

Her arms were shaking, the bar looming over her head like a guillotine. She hated that bar, but goddamnit, she loved it too.

She was halfway down for the final repetition when she knew she couldn't get it back up. Her arms didn't give out, but they informed her that they were tired of her ambition as the weight hovered against her chest.

She looked around the gym, face red from the pressure, trying to find someone to help. All she could see were spots dancing around her vision.

"Jesus!"

Hands clasped either side of hers, an audible grunt of exertion, and suddenly she could breathe. As her vision cleared, Morgan affixed a scowl across her face as Jackson started the lecture.

"How many times do I have to *fucking* tell you to ask for a spotter when you go for a PR Morgan?"

"I was—was fine," she snapped back, but gasping for air didn't make for a very convincing argument.

"You're lucky I was paying attention, did you tear anything?" His hands, which were far colder than Morgan thought was natural, were already examining her shoulders and elbows for bruising.

"I'm *fine* Jackson!"

"Your face says otherwise, looks like the veins in your temples might dye your hair red."

She didn't have anything to say to that.

Jackson turned back to the bench and looked at the weights loaded neatly on the bar.

"190? You were doing 180 like two weeks ago Morgs! Are you *trying* to fucking hurt yourself?!"

Maybe she was, she tried not to think about that too much. After last night she was trying not to think about much of anything.

"I thought I could do it, and I *almost* had it. That was my *last* rep," she felt a little dizzy, like she mig—

"Oh, you're *fucking* kidding me."

Jackson got the trashcan about two seconds too late, managing to catch about half of the protein shake and pre-workout she had chugged an hour before. As he looked at the vomit splattered across the floor, some of which flecked his shoes like rain drops, Morgan saw a brief flash of frustration before he sighed, handing her the can with one of his giant hands before heading to the corner to grab a mop.

"What'd Davy do this time?"

Morgan gritted her teeth and avoided his gaze as he cleaned around her, ringing out the mop in its bucket before getting the disinfectant spray and wiping down the floor and equipment. She only looked up when he handed her a paper towel.

"You got a little..." he mimed wiping to the corner of his mouth.

Morgan cleaned the sick from her face, met his mud brown eyes, and simply said, "He's cheating."

He hid his surprise like a toddler smuggling a cookie from the jar.

"David, the awkward twig with a heart of gold and a head full of dull marbles, is *cheating* on *you*."

She shrugged.

"Did you know?" she asked when the silence stretched too long under the clinical white gym lights.

"Hell no, I'd have whooped his ass. How sure are you?"

The words stuck in her throat at first, then came out fast, like opening a dropped can of soda.

"He's coming home late every other night, texting some woman named 'V,' and he has a key to some stranger's house. He even changed the password on his phone so I couldn't get in."

Jackson sat down at the end of the bench, letting out another sigh and putting a calloused hand to his bald forehead. His taking it seriously somehow made her chest hurt even more. He looked more than just stressed, he almost looked panicked.

"Do you want me to look into it Morgs?"

She looked at him, questioning.

"Pro bono, friends discount. I haven't had a stable fucking case all December anyways."

She hesitated, but before she could even say it he echoed her thoughts.

"I'll be careful Morgan, he's one of my best friends, he won't know shit. He *can't* know shit. Hopefully this is just the result of some lame ass nerd hobby he is embarrassed to tell you about and you're being paranoid…"

Over the next week Morgan contemplated lots of things. She thought about crying, leaving, yelling and committing a multitude of forms of violence. Instead of doing any of those things however, she went to work, came home and watched.

He was being weird. Going to bed early every night, still praying before meals with that stupid necklace.

She wanted to confront him about it, but she just couldn't fathom how to bring it up. Maybe she didn't want to know the answer to what was going on. Maybe she was scared he would get angry like he did last time.

David hadn't been late again all week, but it was Friday.

V: thanks for the meal, same time next week right?

"Same time next week," Morgan muttered under her breath as she pulled into her empty driveway.

The radio in her car reported another girl missing as she sat there, holding together the anger and panic that made her hands feel like jumper cables. Five missing in five weeks made Morgan glad she could put most people on their asses if they tried to fuck with her. She almost wished someone would try.

Three houses away, the LED lights of a black Jeep flared to life and pulled toward her. The tinted passenger window rolled down as it stopped in front of her and David's two-story apartment.

"Are you sure you want to come Morgs?"

"Best to get it over with, right?"

Morgan embraced the steady rainfall of the night, closing her car door and climbing into Jackson's lift kitted Jeep. She rolled her eyes at him as she accepted a much-needed hand to pull her in.

"You do know this isn't the most inconspicuous car for a PI right?"

He smiled, the missing right canine that he fought so hard to conceal from everyone staring at her from the passenger seat.

"Maybe *that's* why I can't get any work unless I offer it for free."

"That's an option, or maybe it's the fact that people around here don't need your help."

"Sure," he said, letting the word drag out, "I think everyone has a skeleton of one size or another in their closet. I think they're just too afraid to shine the bones."

She didn't have anything to say to that, her fingernails bit into her palms as she ignored the streetlights that floated past her like fireflies. Tires on wet asphalt made a solid hum to fill the void in conversation as they made their way towards the heights of the city.

"Whatever he's doing...this certainly isn't the kind of neighborhood I would envision Davy in," Jackson hazarded as multi story mansions scrolled by the windshield.

"How do you even know where we're going?"

He laughed half-heartedly, keeping his eyes on the road, "If I tell you then you might have to testify in court if I get caught, you sure you wanna know?"

Morgan shook her head.

"When'd the guy I had to help set up a printer in college learn to track vehicles?"

Jackson laughed, declining to answer as he flicked off their headlights.

Maybe this was all nothing.

She knew it wasn't.

Jackson pulled the monster mobile over a block and a half away from the house, if that was the right word for residences in the heights. The whole vehicle shuddered as he threw it into park and shut it down.

"Ready to get wet?" he asked, but Morgan was already zipping up her jacket and cinching her hood closed.

Ice cold water splashed over her boots as she dismounted from the behemoth vehicle, and she repressed a full body chill as Jackson took the lead down the dimly lit sidewalk. The pair of them almost certainly looked suspicious, given Jackson's body builder frame and her short and stout silhouette. Jackson had told her to wear black, which wasn't that hard considering it made up a solid 60% of her wardrobe. He was wearing a black jumpsuit with a hoodie over the top, a duffle on his shoulder. Morgan couldn't help but think he looked just a little bit like he belonged in an early 2000's MTV set.

She hoped wealthy people didn't bother looking out windows.

The massive sprawling building whose fence they set up behind made the most lavish structures from her small hometown look positively destitute. A buttressed tower was affixed to the front right corner of the dark wood and stone mansion, the whole thing surrounded by a fence of wrought iron with decorations in freshly polished bronze. The windows leaked faint light from around heavy red curtains, barely visible in the gloom and rain. The gate was closed and sitting behind it, in front of the large ironbound double doors, was an unassuming black sedan.

David's black sedan.

Blood flooded to Morgan's head so fast she thought her heart was going to bust through her ribs and make a big red mess on the finely trimmed rosebush they were ducked behind.

"He certainly isn't *'just working late,'* now, is he?"

Jackson hesitated.

"No, it doesn't look like it… That doesn't mean he's cheating on you though." He squeezed her shoulder gently, which probably would have hurt a bit if she wasn't so upset.

"You're allowed to be mad at him. Either way he's been lying to you Morgs. Let's at least wait and find out what he's doing before we choose the nuclear option though, alright?"

"Do you really think he *isn't* fucking cheating with all this shit Jackson?" Morgan said, annunciating each word carefully and quietly to keep herself from screaming it at him.

"This whole thing seems…odd. I don't know what to think yet. Let's get a little closer."

He reached up to his chest, closing his eyes and grabbing what Morgan assumed were his old dog tags through the fabric of his shirt for good luck. He got on one knee and cupped his hands, offering her a boost over the fence.

"Are you fucking *kidding* me? This is insane Jackson; you tell me not to freak out and then casually offer to trespass on some rich bitch's mansion?"

He shrugged, moving his hands up and down in a "you wanna go or not" gesture.

Morgan looked up at the spikes topping the fence, imagined landing on them, and looked back to Jackson.

"Are you *trying* to make me a kebab?"

"I wouldn't do that."

"Then how do you suppose this will work?"

"Roll when you land, it'll be okay."

He was serious. Seriously crazy. Maybe it said something about her frame of mind that Morgan put her foot in his hands anyways.

Everything around her seemed brighter as even more adrenaline hit her brain like a freight train. Jackson threw her up with a grunt and she was suddenly flying towards the spikes.

She passed the top, curling into a ball to give her ankles the half inch of clearance they needed, and then fell into a clumsy roll on the well maintained lawn, jarring her left shoulder.

"Holy *fuck*," she gasped out, rubbing the shoulder with glass slicked hands.

Jackson was already moving to follow her, putting on some odd-looking gloves and beginning to climb the metal like it was an elementary school's rock wall. He reached the spikes, placed his right foot on a lower cross section, bound up his muscles, and pounced forward like a cat.

He cleared the fence with a good foot and a half of room to spare, coming down in an almost graceful roll that ended with him sliding over a yard in the grass on the seat of his pants.

Morgan stared in slight disbelief.

"Alright," he said, putting the gloves back in his duffle bag, "how far do you want to go?"

Morgan didn't know for sure, hadn't really thought this far ahead.

"I want to know for sure, if we can," she said.

Jackson nodded and got low to the ground, signaling her to follow as he tore off across the shadowed lawn, darting in between decorations and flower bushes with his long legs.

By the time they reached the side of the mansion, Morgan was struggling to keep from audibly panting. She was never really a fan of cardio.

Jackson let her rest against the cool stone for a minute before he peeked his head into an elegant stained glass window covered in some odd looking runes. The instant that he peeked up he ducked back down, as if afraid of being stung.

"*Shit!*"

"*What is it?*" she whispered, far more loudly than she intended to.

He didn't answer, instead grabbing her wrist and pulling her with him back towards the fence.

Morgan was about to protest when overhead lights along the mansion's roof turned the yard into daylight.

"*Fuck!*" Jackson cursed, picking up the pace to the point that Morgan could barely keep from tripping over the ground. They tore down the main driveway now. Somewhere, Morgan heard a large door open.

"I think we're done with subtlety," Jackson said as he let go of her arm, reaching in his pack and bringing out a pair of bolt cutters. He raced ahead of her, covering the distance at a pace that made her realize he'd been barely jogging before. He made it all the way to a big metal box along the fence, delicately hidden by a rose bush. He put the bolt cutters to a thick black cord leaving the bottom of the box and squeezed.

The lights went out, sudden darkness swallowing Morgan's vision. She felt her right foot slip on a rock and she met a dogwood head on, the shrubish tree taking her out at the chest and driving the wind from her lungs.

Blood pounded in her head as she tried to get enough air in to get up and keep running.

Another light shot out of the dark, a flashlight swiveling back and forth across the yard.

"Who—who's there!" David's voice sounded weak and scared.

Morgan, for her part, didn't think.

Breath finally re-entered her lungs and all she felt outside the pain in her chest was a mix of panic and anger. She found one of the rocks she had tripped over, hefted it in her hand, and threw it like a shot put at the flashlight.

"Come ou—" the rock hit David with an audible *fwump* sound and the light fell on the ground.

"We gotta go!" Jackson said, a couple feet to her left.

Morgan threw another rock, this one aimed at where she guessed the back window of David's car should be. Shattering glass and an infantile car alarm sounded like bombs throughout the block.

"God dammit Morgan now isn't the fucking *time*," he whisper-shouted, grabbing her around the waist and throwing her in a fire man's carry as he ran.

Somehow, he had opened the gate amidst the darkness, and as Morgan's eyes finally readjusted, she saw the streetlights coming back into view as Jackson hauled ass back to their wheels.

He set her down unceremoniously when they were a couple houses away, not stopping his running pace as he awkwardly fumbled for his keys in his pants pocket. Morgan ran to the passenger side just as the lights flashed that it was unlocked, climbing up the massive side as quickly as she could. The key turned in the ignition and Jackson began to calmly drive away.

"What are you *doing*? Go faster!" Morgan started slapping the front dash, eyes dashing around for police. They were fucked, they were *so* fucked.

Jackson, besides his chest heaving from the run, looked incredibly calm.

"Hello?!"

He laughed, the sound echoing in the cab of the jeep.

"What about us going to *jail* is funny?!"

"Relax Morgs, we're fine."

Her jaw went slack as she looked at him in disbelief.

"How in *fuck* are we 'fine'?!"

"Closest barracks is on 11th Street, we're in the heights. Rich shitheads didn't want an ugly barracks building detracting from their property value. Police take around 12 and a half minutes to get all the way up here, and that's *if* traffic cooperates." He glanced over at her, smiling like he had when they had all been a bunch of idiot high schoolers skipping physics class.

Morgan tried to get her pulse to settle down and stop leaping out of her throat.

"How the fuck do you know that?"

Jackson kept his eyes on the road.

"It's kind of my job to know. I've worked some cases up here before, thankfully that knowledge never came up till now."

He took them down several alleys until they emerged out onto a main road heading back towards her house.

"So…" she let the word trail off, "what made you start running?"

He didn't answer at first, his boyish smile getting paved over with a frown as he guided them through the dreary city streets.

"A woman. She…she wasn't wearing anything Morgs…I didn't see Davy in there though. But me and the naked woman…we locked eyes."

Morgan's chest felt like the bar was on it again, like 190 pounds of heartache was crushing the life out of her.

"So he real—"

Her phone started ringing, the default tone she'd never bothered changing echoing in the cab of the jeep like church bells.

Jackson jerked the wheel in surprise before pulling the car over to the berm.

"You really fucking went with me sneaking for reconnaissance with your god damn *ringer* on?!" Jackson said, more amazed than angry.

David's face beamed up at Morgan from the phone, **Loves** above it where his name should be. She felt like she was going to pass out.

Jackson seemed to recover from the shock faster than her.

"There's no way he knows Morgan, just answer, act normal."

She thought about letting it go to voicemail, but worry forced her to slide the button over to answer.

"Yes?" she answered, hoping the sound of rain and passing cars didn't get picked up in the background, hoping he couldn't hear her heart pounding through the mic.

"Honey? Hey! Uh, I'm really sorry but I'm gonna be home late—I mean later than I already am! Some, uh, some…stuff came up, and my car ended up getting dinged. I'm okay but I just wanted to give you a heads up."

Dinged was a way to put it.

"Alright, I'll put your food in the microwave, okay?"

"You're the best," he sounded sincere. When had he gotten so good at lying?

"I will see you when I get home honey, I love you," he said.

She wanted to scream.

"You too."

She hung up, tossing her phone on the dash and trying to pull the tears already streaming down her face back into her eyes with her shaking hands.

Jackson was quiet, putting a hand on her knee in an attempt at comforting her as he pulled back into traffic. Morgan had also thought Jackson was a good person, but he had never really been good at dealing with emotions, especially when there weren't any bombastic actions to be taken to help.

They pulled back into her driveway a few minutes later, the jeep seeming like a giant behind her tiny hatchback.

"Uh…do you need anything?" Jackson asked awkwardly.

Morgan shook her head, keeping her eyes facing forward, glued to the front door of their home.

"Okay well…if you do, I'm just a text away. If you need someplace to crash, I have a blow-up mattress you can set up in the living room…"

"Was it proof enough Jackson?"

It was his turn to look forward, avoid her gaze. They sat there for what felt like an age.

"It certainly doesn't look great," he said, pausing before adding, "I'm sorry Morgs."

"Me too."

She undid her seat belt, grabbed the door handle like a pallbearer's swing bar and stepped into the icy rain.

Morgan packed her old army duffle, having already filled a suitcase with eight years' worth of a life with someone. Her clothes were crushed together to fit, some old stuff she hadn't worn in years shoved in the trash can she had brought up from the kitchen.

Some things she could come back for, but she knew she wouldn't, or rather *couldn't* be here when David got back tonight.

She wasn't crying anymore, choosing to let the physical monotony of picking things up and putting them in the duffle act as a comfortable Band-Aid of static over the open wound that was her world falling apart. She finished in the bathroom before moving to the bookshelf that stood to the ceiling in their bedroom. Former bedroom.

Morgan only really had a couple books there, which she hadn't read yet, alongside a half dozen journals she'd filled over the years. The first journal was worn and water stained from the time David had accidentally flipped their canoe over on their second date. She flipped through some of the stuck together pages, finding old horror movie tickets and cheap, paper fair bracelets.

She closed it and set back on the shelf, afraid it would burn her if she held it too long.

She was putting the last of the other 5 journals in her bag when she noticed something.

On the third oaken shelf there was a trio of books that had no doubt seen more use than the rest. The Lord of the Rings stared at Morgan from below her—the second book missing its tattered book cover. She pulled it off the shelf and leafed through it, finding crumbs and formerly dog-eared pages. Her pulse quickened.

Morgan set the book down on the shelf, rushing around the lonely king mattress to David's nightstand. The book cover for The Two Towers hung like an oversized winter coat on the book sitting atop the dew-ring-stained nightstand. Morgan lifted the book, peeling off the cover to reveal a pitch-black exterior with no words, only a peculiar looking design of a bright red "V" surrounded in unintelligible scribbles.

The pages flipped by as Morgan thumbed through it, confusion and panic mixing in her chest. The text was all written—handwritten—in brownish red ink, symbols she couldn't identify accompanied illustrations of strange circles. Morgan half assumed it to be some odd prop until the faint smell of iron hit her nostrils as the pages whirred by. Blood.

Fear crept into her sinuses to greet the unpleasant smell when she reached an engraved metal bookmark with David's name on it, the one she'd gotten him for his birthday last year.

The page before her had yet another strange circle, accompanied by a crude outline of a woman's silhouette with runes lined over different parts of her body. Obscuring the linework in the center of the page was a red splotch of vibrant, *fresh* blood which had smudged the surrounding text.

"Holy *fuck* David…"

Morgan ran downstairs, skipping steps as she rushed out the door. Her keys were in her hands and she was almost to her car when she finally had the sense to turn around and pick up her phone.

"Jackson! David's in trouble, *big trouble*! I think he's about to do something stupid. That woman you saw is in *danger*," she panted as she tried to use one hand to open the door to their garage.

"What do you mean Morgan? Slow down I can ha—"

"I can't explain it all right now, just meet me there okay? Get the police too, I'm already on my way!"

"Morgan you can *not* go there I—"

"I'm already leaving, we have to *hurry!*"

She tried to hang up, but the rain had made her phone slippery and it shot out of her grip and into a puddle by the gutter spout.

"Fucking *dammit!*" she screamed, leaving the undoubtedly ruined phone and instead wrenching up the garage door.

The place was cluttered, filled with all of David's car junk for the shitty old Mustang he had said he was going to restore a few years ago. Morgan picked her way through the mess and got to the back corner where their camping stuff was stashed. She tore into the bags, finding bear mace and the ax they used to chop firewood when they had gone on overnight hikes all those years ago. She clipped the mace to a belt loop and gingerly swung the eight-pound ax head up and onto her shoulder.

The loose belt in Morgan's car squealed at her as she shot out of their driveway and up towards the heights.

She just hoped she'd get there in time.

The gate was still open at the mansion. Morgan contemplated driving in, but she decided on parking a block away when she saw Jackson's jeep there, pulling behind it. There was no sign of Jackson himself other than steam from the rain hitting the hood of the car. Morgan could only assume he had beaten her there and was already headed inside. Alone.

"*Fucking idiot,*" she cursed under her breath before taking off towards the mansion.

The streetlights made the rain look like motes of falling glass all around her as she tried her best to look inconspicuous carrying an ax on the sidewalk in a rich neighborhood. The lights lining the top of the massive house were still out, though Morgan didn't know if that was because of Jackson's sabotage or if they had simply turned them off.

David's back window had been roughly protected from the elements by some trash bags and duct tape.

The dark wooden double doors loomed over Morgan as she knelt behind the car, taking a moment to think things through. The police should be there soon. It had been eight minutes already. Maybe she should wait.

Jackson was already inside.

What if they weren't fast enough?

Morgan flew into motion, crossing the distance between the car and the front door faster than she had known she was capable of. She jiggled the doorknob, fully prepared to make her own entry with the ax if she had to, but found it unlocked. The rightmost door clicked and glided soundlessly open, revealing a long-furnished hallway, lit only by the streetlights outside beyond the fence.

Creepy.

Morgan went into the house ready to hit the first thing that moved near her. She heard the sound of voices, muffled, deeper inside. She headed towards them, trying her best not to make any noise on the old wooden floor. All the magnificent details of paintings and candelabras were hidden in a blurry fuzz by the darkness of the place, a darkness that seemed to eat away at Morgan the further she went.

There were doorways every few feet, leading into some different more ostentatious rooms. Morgan counted two separate libraries, a sitting room, and some sort of art gallery, and those were just the things she noticed.

That and the smell, like roadkill on a back road.

She stayed in the main hall, picking up the faintest bit of flickering light peeking out from under a door twenty feet away, towards the back of the house. The voices were louder now. One of them was David's.

"Are we good to start?"

When she was fifteen feet away, she heard the antique knob turning.

Morgan spun into one of the rooms, gently closing the door to all but a crack in an attempt to hide from whatever was on its way. She nearly lost her cool as her hand stuck to the doorknob, which was covered in some substance she couldn't make out in what was now almost total darkness.

She did her best to suppress a gag as the smell of the room washed over her.

Large, heavy footsteps walked slowly down the hallway she'd just been in. Her grip threatened to splinter the handle of the fire ax. They were too loud to be David. Her heart beat so hard she could taste the iron of it in the back of her throat.

The footsteps passed.

She eased the door open, using the nearly extinct light from the street to stare into the deep shadows of her hiding place. In the corner, there was an uneven pile of odd shapes. She made out a foot, separated from the rest of its owner.

Morgan counted two dozen rushed seconds before she darted back into the hallway and away from the bodies, closing on the door at the end that now stood ajar, letting a ribbon of candlelight bathe the hall like a brushstroke.

Reaching the doorway, she saw David standing at the edge of a circle of lit candles, intricate lines of indecipherable text etched in fresh blood between and around them on the floor like hellish spiderwebs. His hand held a pocketknife, the same one he had once used to whittle marshmallow roasting sticks for them.

It was covered in blood.

The woman, also covered in blood, lay naked in the middle of the circle.

Morgan pushed the door the rest of the way open, its hinges creaking faintly.

"We all g—"

When he saw her he froze, stunned, his too-small eyes going wide in their shrimpy sockets.

He raised the knife in caution.

"Easy Morgan…I don't know what you're doing here but I don't want to hurt yo—"

Morgan felt her knuckles dislocate his jaw.

She had closed the distance in three quick steps, her left fist catching him in the chin before he could react.

Still reeling from the first blow, David lashed out with the knife at her. She leapt back, then jumped forward again, bringing the blunt top of the ax into his sternum with her right hand like a spear.

There was a crackling sound as it broke ribs, and he crumpled bonelessly to the ground, knocking several candles over, their liquid wax extinguishing them.

"What the fucking *hell*!" she screamed down at him. He didn't respond.

She didn't know what else to do.

Inside the circle, the naked woman was beginning to wake. Her body was covered in more symbols, lines drawn across light brown skin in bright red blood. The same lines and symbols from the book.

Morgan rushed to her, dropping the ax to peel off her own black zip-up and drape it over the woman's shoulders.

"Are you okay?"

The woman merely looked at her, seemingly confused. She was beautiful. Blood ran from the top crown of runes between her eyes, around her nose and down to her lips.

She licked them, smiling up at Morgan with sharp, pointed teeth.

"Dinner?" she asked in a low voice, like a millstone grinding bones.

Morgan jumped away, kicking more candles across the floor as she backpedaled for the door. She hit something, a person, and turned her fall into a dive to the left behind a red leather couch as she tried to gain distance.

Standing in the doorway, was a towering figure, wide shoulders bound in a black jumpsuit.

"Jackson, run! She isn't what she looks like!" Morgan screamed as she looked back towards the monster. The nightmare had its long, bloody fingernails pressed against the air marked by the circle, as if trying to push against it, leaning on nothing, somehow trapped inside.

"I think it's stuck in there, we sho—"

"I'm sorry Morgs."

Morgan stilled, the adrenaline running through her curdling and replacing itself with a deep-set dread.

She turned to look at Jackson in the doorway. His face was lit by the remaining candles, shoulders bunched up and together, jaw clenched and eyes staring at his feet, refusing to meet hers. David lay a few steps away from him, still out cold. Jackson leaned down and picked up the fire ax lying beside him.

"This wasn't how it was supposed to go. I tried to get you to leave…"

Morgan got to her feet, backing towards the bookshelves that lined the walls of the room. The monster kept trying to tear through the circle, staring at her and clacking its razor-sharp teeth together, Morgan's jacket falling to the ground covered in blood from its shoulders.

Jackson took a step toward Morgan.

"J—Jackson what are you on about, let's get out of here…" Her voice was wavering, she looked for windows, other doors, anywhere to run. Jackson kept himself between her and the only exit as he approached.

"I'm sorry." His hand pulled the amulet from under his shirt, holding it tightly in his left fist. The silvery metal glinted at her in the candlelight, almost laughing at her. The humanity leaked from his eyes, leaving something cold in their place.

"I know you don't understand. If you could see what she has shown me, what she showed *us*."

His hand was red when he released the amulet, small metal spines on its rim drank in his blood greedily.

Morgan hesitated as he continued to close the distance, weighing her fear of him and the seemingly trapped monster. She kept backing up, coming closer to the now steady sound of saliva dripping onto the wooden floor behind her.

"Jackson, you don't have to do this…"

Tears began to run down his cheeks, but he kept walking forward.

"I didn't want to, no," his breath frosted the air in front of him, "you should have just left Morgan."

Morgan was now fully around the monster, having passed around the beast's circle, feeling its breath on her neck, until her back was pinned in the corner of the room, Jackson looming over her.

Behind him, the monster mewed, "*Dinner* Jackson, *feed* Vorticalia, I **hunger**!"

The ax raised over his head, the mass of him more than Morgan had any hope of moving.

"I'm so sorry Morgan," he said again, eyes closing in a silent prayer.

When he opened his eyes to bring the ax down, Morgan squeezed the trigger on the bear mace.

The liquid lanced up to his forehead before she pulled the stream down into his eyes and nose.

Jackson screamed, an awful high-pitched sound. Recoiling, he dropped the ax and backed away from the stream, which was still flowing from the canister. His leg caught the side of a couch, and he tumbled, one arm wheeling while the other clawed at his face.

He landed in the outstretched arms of Vorticalia.

She looked down at him sympathetically for a second before her serrated teeth tore through his neck like a hole puncher.

Morgan stood frozen, finger still pulling the trigger of the now empty can of mace.

The thing ate, moving from the neck to the strong shoulders even as Jackson's body continued to twitch. The remaining candles that had made up the circle were scattered; several had rolled across the room and Morgan smelled paper kindling as a bookshelf began to smoke.

Shaking with shock, she took a slow step along the perimeter of the room, trying to let the monster focus on its meal—on fucking *Jackson*—the can of mace falling from her hand to the carpeted floor.

The blood shot eyes darted to her, a smile spreading across gore smeared lips.

The thing let the remains of Jackson's limp body slump to the ground, taking a cautious step, crossing the threshold that the candles had kept in place. Whatever power had been there seemed to have broken with the circle.

The smile grew wider, as if teeth were growing in to more thoroughly fill out its hideous mouth.

"Food?" it asked, the deep voice coming from the woman's petite form was filled with bloody phlegm.

Morgan kept moving, resisting the urge to run and taking calm, confident steps. She knew deep down that the thing was faster than her.

"*Food?*" it asked again, more insistently, closing the distance between them.

There was no way out.

"*FOOD!*" Vorticalia's voice went from a deep rumble to a high-pitched scream as she bolted across the room towards Morgan.

Morgan caught the things outstretched hands as it lunged for her, interlocking their fingers.

She took a step back, leaning on her left leg and lifting her right as she spun, keeping her arms extended and using the beast's speed to pick it up and off the ground, throwing it towards the bookshelves behind her.

Vorticalia didn't want to let go, digging her claws into Morgan's hands. Morgan screamed in pain, but the physics were in her favor. The naked woman's grip faltered and she flew into the tower of books, snapping two of the middle shelves cleanly in half, their contents raining down on top of her.

Morgan, hands dripping blood on the floor from the ragged tears through her skin, turned to run. Smoke filled the air with a haze as fire licked up the sides of a wall now. The pile of books on the floor began to catch fire as Vorticalia rose from amongst them.

She screamed, Morgan screamed too, their voices accompanied by the undercurrent of crackling flames.

Morgan's back was turned, but she knew she wouldn't outrun it, so she grabbed the ax from where Jackson had dropped it.

Vorticalia was on her in an instant, unnaturally fast. Morgan brought the ax in a spinning uppercut as she stood, using the muscles in her legs and back to drive the force.

The ax buried itself in the monster's right armpit, lifting it off its feet a few inches and halting its momentum. Morgan tried to hack the arm clean off, but her hands slipped on her own blood and lost their grip. Vorticalia reached her other claw towards Morgan's face while Morgan's arms were still over her head from the swing.

She brought both her fists down on the top of Vorticalia's head with a scream.

David's monster crumbled like a limp ragdoll to the floor, the ax handle sticking out of it up towards the ceiling.

Morgan didn't have time to relax, the smoke filling the room burned her lungs. She lurched towards where David lay, unconscious. She slapped him.

"We gotta *go!*" she screamed.

He woke, shaking his head in pain as she helped him up.

She started pulling him towards the exit as the fire wrapped the ceiling overhead. His eyes stared behind her as he gained his wits.

He broke from her grip.

She turned, confused, panicked, only to see him walk into the inferno.

"*David!*"

He bent down, fire eating away at his skin as he gently cradled the monster's corpse in his arms.

He didn't even look at her as tears boiled on his face.

Morgan left him, running through the fire that licked at her shoulders, running from what had once been love.

The police arrived exactly 12 and a half minutes after the rich neighbors called them to report a woman carrying a fire ax breaking into the abandoned house next door.

They found Morgan sitting by the fence gate, the mansion lighting up the night behind her as flames licked at the remnants of her life.

Her hands were no longer bleeding, cauterized by the white-hot door handles she'd had to turn on her way out, her black hair was singed down close to her scalp and her clothes were spotted with holes.

Morgan didn't cry, didn't shake or weep. She merely sat in the ash spattered rain, staring at the darkened sky with the icy dread of someone who wished she had just kept eating cold food.

By letting go of control, a mess can come together. Remember those Magic Eye illusions?

My local mall used to have a funky store that featured all sorts of tchotchkes and gifts, including those Magic Eye posters. They advertised them by having a sample or two hung on the wall next to the display. As a kid, I'd stare at that absolute graphic mess and try to will the magic into my eyeballs. Other customers would exclaim, "a sailboat!" and I'd nod and grin and pretend that I also saw a sailboat instead of a repetitive splatter of splotches and blobs.

People tried to help me.

"Stand really close to it, then back up slowly," they'd say. "That's the trick."

It wasn't.

"Unfocus your eyes!" they'd encourage. "Don't look at the pattern, look *through* the pattern."

It was hopeless. No amount of well-intentioned instruction worked. All I saw was the bottom of a pigpen after 80s night on the farm. Then, one day, one magical afternoon at the mall, someone suggested I take off my glasses and try again. I stepped back from the poster, glasses in hand, and fought as my eyes tried and failed to focus on the chaotic pop-art tangle in front of me. One step back, another step back, and viola! There it was. The sailboat. For a brief, fleeting moment I glimpsed the 3-D image hidden among the blobs, before my eyes gave up and refocused into the blur of color.

Sometimes, when I'm trying to solve a puzzle, I think about those Magic Eye things. I tried so many different ways to see the illusion, but it hadn't occurred to me to remove my glasses. Why would I? I use my glasses to see, and I was trying to see something.

Wasn't I?

The trick was that I didn't just need to see it, I needed to see it differently, and I've learned that some of the most satisfying puzzles to solve ask the same thing of me.

So, dear puzzler, if you get stuck—maybe try removing your proverbial glasses.

A Lady's Work Is Never Done

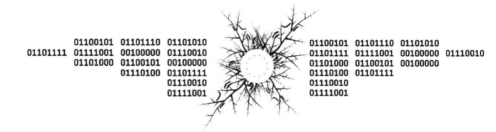

01100101 01101110 01101010
01101111 01111001 00100000 01110010
01101000 01100101 00100000
01110100 01101111
01110010
01111001

01100101 01101110 01101010
01101111 01111001 00100000 01110010
01101000 01100101 00100000
01110100 01101111
01110010
01111001

BY TRACEY LANDER-GARRETT

We all told Johnny that his house renovation project was going to be a money pit—an aged Victorian by the river— "With a history!" he explained—but none of us imagined the danger lurking there—no one thought things like that happened outside of movies.

The house had belonged to a bootlegger whose bathtub gin made the journeys to Pittsburgh and points beyond back in the Prohibition days, later becoming a house of ill repute sometime after the bootlegger died.

Johnny was new to town and raising his six-year-old daughter Sara alone. Weekdays, he worked construction and Sara went to school. On Sunday mornings and food distribution days they came to our Parish Church, St. Elizabeth's.

Johnny came into our food pantry. He wore jeans and those yellow construction boots and a heavy canvas jacket—all solid colors on a solid man. Tall, but not so tall he had to hunch beneath the beams like Father Pulaski. Sara barely came up to his hip. A little willowy thing, with big brown eyes and chin-length brown hair. She clung to her daddy's hand and yessirred and no ma'amed us all in the sweetest way and you know our deacon Tom threw in an extra box of cookies because she looked like she needed feeding up. And we'd known them for a few months like that, and she was the same every time.

They moved into the house in February, a rainy snowy season here in the Midwest of the Northeast, which is to say both and neither, but it was gray, and overcast, and cold, and there wasn't much for little Sara to do in the house while her father worked construction—besides watch her Frozen DVD over and over again—at least that's what we told ourselves when she began acting out.

The next time they came in after moving into that house—Sara was wearing one of those long blonde wigs the little girls wear for Halloween—this time she was like a different child, pouting and crossing her arms and pursing her lips, saying Anna this, and Anna that. *No, Anna hates blueberries,* pout. *We need an extra one for Anna. Anna loves peaches. Anna says ladies don't eat sweets.* Anna etcetera.

"Who's Anna, Sara?" asked Tom, filling up their bags.

"Anna says a lady don't speak to a gentleman she don't know his name," Sara said with a toss of her head, the wig's long blonde tresses flipped over her shoulder. It was an odd movement on a child, somehow adult and coy.

Tom laughed, surprised. "Is that so?" He put his hands on his hips and smiled at her, and Sara crossed her arms and turned her face away.

"Anna is Sara's imaginary friend," Johnny mumbled from the side of his mouth, like he half didn't want Sara to hear.

"Ohhhh, you have a new friend," Tom said. "Where'd you meet her?"

"Hmph!" said Sara. It was kind of cute, but also strange.

"Sara, what happened to your hair?" I asked.

"Anna says short hair is for old ladies."

Considering my own pixie cut at the time, I found this remark somewhat rude.

"Anna seems to have a lot of opinions," I said.

"You don't know the half of it," said Johnny, and he sounded weary. He looked weary, too, now that I took a closer look at him. Unshaven, his eyes bloodshot.

"Johnny, can we bring anything over? Help you with the new place?"

"That's kind of you, but—well—" His eyes flitted over his daughter. "I really think she could use a *real* friend?"

We made play date arrangements and I brought my daughter Phoenix over to their house after her soccer practice. We brought cookies and a bottle of cabernet and Phoenix went upstairs to Sara's room to play while the adults opened the wine.

Glasses of wine in hand, Johnny gave me a tour of the renovations he'd been up to and only about half of the house was livable, with the other half essentially a construction site: rooms barely framed out with hanging wires and stacks of sheetrock in the corner.

We talked about the upcoming rummage sale and had some single parent relatable moments, but I never got the feeling he was—I mean, it had only been a few months since his wife had died and I wasn't expecting anything—but then Phoenix appeared in the doorway, just sort of out of breath slightly, and said, "Mom, can we go?" and behind her stood Sara, Sara in her long blonde wig, with this hand mirror, an antique silver ladies hand mirror, like something out of a period movie. Her lips puckered in a pout as she gazed at herself in the mirror, wrapping one platinum curl around a finger.

"Ladies always brush their hair one hundred times a day," Sara lisped. Then she giggled and put her hand on her daddy's arm.

It was wrong.

It was wrong and awful and yet there was nothing so awful about what she said, or even, really, the way she said it, except that it was all just wrong.

She just wasn't the same child.

"A lady's work is never done. Ain't that so?" Sara insisted.

"You see?" Johnny whispered.

"Mom. Let's *go*," Phoenix said, her hand clammy in mine, tugging insistently.

The therapist at the free clinic our vicar Tom recommended told Johnny that forming an imaginary friendship was a normal childhood coping mechanism. That the trauma of losing a parent, then the isolation following a big move was very likely what had brought on this change. A little weekly chat and crayon therapy and soon Sara would be back to her old self.

But a month later, Sara's symptoms were worse. It had gotten so that she would only answer to Anna. Anna dictated every choice and decision. Oatmeal three meals a day. She would only wear long dresses. The long blond wig was a constant.

When Johnny found Sara trying to light a curtain on fire because Anna said she must, he said he couldn't take it anymore. The therapist agreed they should try medication, but the child psychiatrist only came into the clinic every other month.

Then came the day that Johnny renovated the basement and excavated the floor, uncovering the skeleton of a young woman. When her remains were moved, buried in a mound of pale blonde hair they found a tarnished silver locket, inscribed ANNA.

The medical examiner estimated she had been there a long time, possibly a hundred years, back to the Prohibition times. She had most certainly been murdered.

Johnny moved them out the next day. We never heard from them again.

My cousin Susan was a realtor and took me to look at the house when it went on the market. Our footsteps echoed eerily on the wood floors. It sounded like someone walking overhead, a crazy ricochet of sound bouncing off the ceiling, we said.

When we went down to the basement, we found that antique silver mirror face down on the steps. When I picked it up to look, my shattered reflection stared back.

I gasped.

"Jan, what is it?" Susan asked, her eyes wide

In the cracked shards of mirror that remained, I caught a glimpse, just a glimpse, of another life, another face.

"Call me Anna," I heard myself say.

"Very funny," Susan said.

"Funny is as funny does," I drawled.

She turned away, like they always do.

Never saw the mirror coming. Oh, how she bled. So much to clean up.

But then a lady's work is never done.

So, I'm a big believer in breakfast food. As in, I believe any food is breakfast food if you eat it first thing in the morning.

Sure, there's something to be said about tradition. Eggs, toast, and bacon are such popular breakfast foods that when some people have that meal at a different time of day, they'll call it "breakfast for dinner." I'd argue that the meal name really is more about the time of day and not necessarily the food consumed.

While I do appreciate a perfectly cooked slice of crispy bacon, there's plenty of room in that morning time for other processed meats to shine. If breakfast sandwiches are something you like, why not fully cross that sandwich threshold? Whether you call it a sub, a hoagie, or a grinder, a big old sandwich teeming with veggies and topped with a good quality olive oil can be excellent fuel for your day.

Cold pizza is a ubiquitous (although somewhat controversial) breakfast choice here in the US, and one you've perhaps tried. If that's something that appeals to you, might I suggest a slice of lasagna for breakfast? Those lovely flavors of tomato and basil and oregano will have comingled with all that cheese overnight, then when reheated, gains a slightly more stable texture. I'd highly recommend it.

And finally, there's the sweet breakfast category. Lots of people will enjoy a muffin on occasion as part of their breakfast, and if that's something you can get behind, then what's stopping you from diving straight into a hunk of birthday cake? Think of how lovely that colorful leftover cake would be with your morning coffee.

Maybe some of you have read this and thought, "gee, Amanda, I care about my health. I'll stick to my regularly scheduled, traditional eggs and bacon." Remember, I support eating whatever you want for breakfast. But for those touting their health as the reason, let me just gently suggest you look into the nutritional value of bacon.

THE LAST CASE

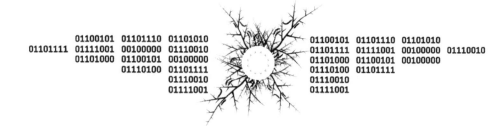

01100101 01101110 01101010
01101111 01111001 00100000 01110010
01101000 01100101 00100000
01110100 01101111
01110010
01111001

01100101 01101110 01101010
01101111 01111001 00100000 01110010
01101000 01100101 00100000
01110100 01101111
01110010
01111001

BY SCOTT RICHARDS

"It's so strange to see his chair empty. Seems impossible, doesn't it?"

Jim turned his head an inch to see the old housekeeper. She lingered in the doorway, years of routine no doubt compelling the preparation of a favourite supper that would never be eaten again. "I think we both know he'd have several opinions on the use of that word."

They shared a smile. The kind burdened by grief, betraying a thousand words that would settle unsaid on the room like dust.

"The Inspector called for you again earlier, Jim. I told him you were in a morose mood and needed time, but I have a feeling he'll be knocking again soon."

"I'd expect nothing else." Jim stared through the flames dancing without a melody in the hearth. "After all, I was the last one to see our friend alive. Or, second to last. I dare say I should be high on his list of suspects."

"Well, forgive me but I'd say that was an offense. And I don't think that's why he wants to see you."

"Innocent men don't feel offense," said Jim. "Only comfort in the firm grip of righteous fact." Jim wondered on how many occasions in the three days since Harmen's death he'd heard the man's words escape his own lips, as though he were still being taught from beyond the veil of death. If there was any mind so stubborn as to resist the inconvenience of the grave, it belonged to Baxter Harmen.

"You haven't seen, have you?" Mrs Walmley produced a newspaper from under her arm and smoothed it out in front of Jim.

SCOTLAND YARD CATCH DETECTIVE KILLER: CASE CLOSED

Jim studied the headline. "Perhaps the inspector wanted to share the news with me himself."

"At least we can let Baxter rest now. You can afford yourself the same."

"Good night, Mrs Walmley." Jim charged his brandy glass. He knew she meant well, but there was too much an air of convenience about the whole scenario. "I shall visit the Inspector tomorrow, regardless. I should like the details of this arrest. However, there is someone that I should seek out first."

Jim pulled the blue cotton handkerchief from his top pocket and wiped a layer of morning dew from the modest bronze plaque that greeted all and sundry to the 'Adelaide Harmen Home for Displaced Children.' Satisfied, he walked around the locked front entrance and into the narrow alley that twisted behind the building.

Jim wrapped a knuckle against the heavy old door, flakes of green paint coming away with his hand.

From inside came a muffled mixture of muted foul language and keys jangling, until the door swung open. Jim took a step back as a wave of hot air escaped.

"Oh, it's just you Jim. I thought you might be stopping by, considering recent events. I'll let the lady of the house know you're here."

"If it's all the same Bert, I'd rather approach her directly. We have sensitive matters to discuss."

Bert removed his flat cap and used it to wave Jim inside. Less than a minute in the kitchen, with the furnace being fed and pots already bubbling, was enough to cause a sweat under the brim of his hat.

He nodded with as much politeness to blank unfamiliar faces as he could muster, before escaping into the rear winding stairwell that would take him up to Adelaide's office.

Recovering his composure and breath after the climb, Jim went over the thousand conversations he'd had in his head with the woman behind that door. Even in his imagination, none of them went favourably.

"You can stop loitering out there. I can hear your moustache bristling."

Even insulted, Jim couldn't help but smile at her biting delivery. An adolescence spent in hopes of becoming a theatre darling had left her with a flair for the dramatic that never fell short. She could have been anything she wanted, only a fool couldn't see that.

"Adelaide," Jim spoke as he stepped in, feeling like a naughty child summoned to the headmaster's office.

She had her back to him, looking out of the window into the city as the sun climbed, dragging the morning along with it.

"Have you come to comfort me, I wonder? Like you used to, so often?"

Jim removed his hat, an empty gesture of gentlemanly conduct in a world that wasn't playing by such arbitrary rules. "A widow and a widower, seeking solace in common ground."

"When did you become so cold? When I lay in your arms, warm and safe. That was not cold. What happened to you? Did all those years with my brother shave away any sense of emotion, my love?"

My love. The words lit his heart with a fire of joy that he so badly wanted to stoke and yet, he could not. He couldn't tell her. Duty and a promise told long ago, strangled his heart's desires. "We were both grieving, then."

"Are we both not grieving now?"

Greif seemed too small a word, drowned out by feelings he lacked the composure to articulate. "No doubt you have seen the headlines. I shall visit the Inspector later on."

"And your fear that their incompetence has led them to an easy arrest, to quell public outcry?"

"I fear a man who bested the greatest mind any of us have any known, out there somewhere unseen."

"How quaint that you assume it to be a man."

"Forgive me. It was merely a turn of phrase."

Adelaide turned away from the light, her eyes usually fizzing with energy were dull and lifeless.

"Jim. Please. You are standing six feet from me but you may as well be a world away.

Why do you insist on this distance?"

I don't. *He* did. He had. Jim had wondered, hoped even, that in the days since Baxter's death, whether some secret will or note might reveal itself and free him from the oath he had taken. It would be so simple, to take a few steps forward and hold Adelaide in his arms once again. He looked at her, at sad crystal tears framing her eyes. It was impossible not to ponder whether she held the same hopes, too. He wanted to ask and yet, the words formed but were not permitted a chance to be heard. Duty moulded them into something else entirely. "I will find the culprit," he heard himself say. "The true culprit. You have my word."

"You gave me that before, too. And look where we are."

"There is a case to be solved, Adelaide. It would be the utmost insult to your brother's memory for me to put anything else before that."

"You sound just like him."

The acknowledgment caused Jim discomfort that he hadn't expected. He respected Baxter, he loved him like one loves a brother in arms. Yet, he had never wanted to be him. Baxter had lived above them all, a mind cursed to solving human trifles but always a few steps removed from the rest of mankind. Jim had no such pretensions of ethereal greatness, but who was he without principles?

"Let us hope that I can think like him." More words that he recognised purely because they were in his voice, and yet he found it hard to believe them, in himself. Hoping to think like Baxter was like hoping to grow wings and fly like a sparrow.

Jim blinked at his pocket watch, putting it to his ear as he was sure it was making a mockery of time. Not yet a half hour after nine yet he felt as though he had been awake for a week. A thick fog lay squat on the ground, a damp grotesque gargoyle that chilled his bones. Still, he was keen to get through this particular appointment and begin the business of solving the case. The case. That was it, don't be attached, don't be emotional. Only the facts mattered, only the truth. Jim sidestepped around a young boy on a unicycle, handing out leaflets advertising a visiting circus. He rode in circles around a tall, thin clown who blew screeching bursts of noise on a flute. The clown fixed Jim with a stare that made him uneasy.

"Ready for the show?"

The clown spoke in a ridiculous voice. Jim shook off the words in his head, eyes scanning the page out of politeness. It promised a variety of wonders, colourful characters, and amazing feats of daring. Taking a pinch of snuff to steady his nerves, Jim climbed the stairs up to Scotland Yard.

The inspector paced back and forth behind his desk, one hand fiddling behind his broad back and another combing his moustache, a bristling broom end of hair perched on his lip.

"Never thought I'd see the day. Thought he'd outlive us all, to be honest with you. He seemed more than mortal."

Jim studied the Inspector's movement. He had no pencil or scrap of paper but his mind scribbled details. See everything. The smallest hint could be your biggest clue. He could hear Baxter's voice. It was getting stronger and louder. Insistent.

"Well, that I can't argue with." He pulled a wad of Baxter's own mixed tobacco from a pouch and wedged it down into his pipe before flicking a match into life.

"It seems impossible that he could be murdered," said the Inspector. "A man like him, bleeding to death in some filthy alleyway. His pockets emptied. That Limehouse wretch that we caught will hang for this."

Jim said nothing in immediate repost but raised an eyebrow as he took a deep draw from his pipe. The urge to reply as Baxter might be bothering him more than he let himself admit. He chewed on an answer like a particularly stubborn toffee.

"For god's sake," said The Inspector, red faced and hands on hips. "Just spit it out, man."

"Baxter disliked the term 'impossible' intensely," said Jim. "As though something unexplainable was an affront to his intelligence. Not that I ever did confront him about it, but there was a disdain in his eyes whenever I said it. A disappointment."

The Inspector let out a dry chuckle. "Yes. He looked at me that way often. He may have been a genius, but he was cold. A coldness that frightened me at times, in all honesty. There is a fine line between genius and madness after all."

Jim tried to hide a visceral reaction to the Inspector's statement. A part of him wanted to agree with the Inspector's assessment, but once more he hid behind formality. "I have to confess; I find it curious that the case seems to have been solved without much in the way of a thorough investigation."

"Men in positions much higher than mine wanted this solved, so it is solved." The Inspector's tone carried more acid now. "The public needs someone to blame for this. Baxter Harmen was a myth, a larger-than-life legend. It's as though someone killed the damn Scarlet Pimpernel."

"So not only could the true killer be at large, but an innocent man could pay for his crime."

"There's nothing innocent about them. We found him in some opium den, rags covered in blood and a knife in the side of his boot."

The Inspector pushed a piece of paper over the desk toward Jim. Cold, clinical details of Baxter's demise. The coroner had recorded the cause of death as loss of blood from three stab wounds to the back. Baxter's voice spoke with clarity inside of his mind. Question everything. His eyes continued down and recorded a note of interest. 'Green substance under fingernails.' Jim filed the fact away in the box of possibilities stacking up in his mind, trying to build a picture of his friend's final moments.

"As you know Inspector, Baxter had physical reflexes as quick as his mind. Had he been so inclined, he could have been a champion boxer or master martial artist."

"Yes." The Inspector rubbed his chin. "I was made aware of that during that whole nasty business with those dogs."

"Baxter would not be caught unawares by some common thief, even if he himself were under the influence."

"What's your point?"

Jim stood, straightening his jacket and putting out his pipe with the thick scared skin of his left thumb. "If anyone got close enough to stab him in the back, there can be only one likely conclusion. It was someone he was comfortable letting get that close. And that list is really rather short."

"Are you on that list?"

"I should be," Jim said with a cold certainty.

"Despite what Baxter thought of my skill, I'm not an idiot. I'm well aware of the convenience of the killer being caught with a murder weapon when someone wanted him to be."

"Perhaps it is not a public outcry someone wanted to avoid. Perhaps it is to cover their own guilt. This may run deeper than either of us would care to think about."

The Inspector hung his head. "Damn it. I can't stop the wheels already in motion. But I can turn the other way if you want to start asking a few quiet questions. Just make sure there is an emphasis on the quiet."

"I need a name," said Jim. "Don't speak it. Just write it down for me. Who tipped you off as to the whereabouts of this apparent murderer?"

The Inspector crumpled into his chair with a sigh and scribbled something with a stub of pencil on a scrap of paper. "The irony isn't lost on me, Jim. I mean no offense but we both know there is one man we'd want on this case and it's his body lying in the morgue. We need a dead man to solve his own murder. How's that for impossible?"

Jim nodded. He couldn't very well confess to Mrs Walmley, Adelaide, the Inspector or anyone else that he felt inadequate. His feelings were complex, too much for an old soldier to put into words inside his mind, never mind out loud. He felt an edge of resentment toward Baxter for putting him in this position and then felt ridiculous for allowing those thoughts to form at all.

The fog had lifted somewhat as Jim left Scotland Yard. The Inspector was rattled. Jim checked the name on the note and folded it back into his pocket. Had he named a thousand possible names, he still wouldn't have arrived at that one. How did that person have so much influence from so far away? He needed to speak to an old friend, but that would have to wait for now as his thoughts were interrupted by a growl from his stomach. The morning had been long and he had yet to take breakfast.

Jim's head swam as he made his way along Westminster Bridge. A cooling wind rising from the Thames made a game of stealing his hat but he managed to reach out and grab it before it became a brief guest on the river's surface. The boy on the unicycle rode past him.

"How about it mister? See the trapeze? The World's strongest woman? The amazing shadow men of mystery?"

"Perhaps another time, son. I'm afraid I have little time for fun at the moment."

Jim tossed him a coin to dissuade further conversation and continued on.

An hour had passed and Jim's stomach had gone from growling to straining against his shirt buttons. It had been an agreeable brunch of sausage, bacon, eggs and coffee. Eating alone at one of their usual spots seemed odd, as though he'd be always looking for Baxter to walk in and fill the seat opposite. He had chosen somewhere on a whim, the warming inviting aroma of hot meats catching his attention.

A young waiter who looked as though he may struggle to carry a single bowl of soup approached him from the side, a parcel tucked under his arm.

"Excuse me Sir, are you Jim Whitmore?"

Jim slid a hand under his jacket and onto the handle of his revolver. "I am."

"This was left here for you, we think. The man who left it was very specific about your appearance."

The waiter held out the package, which Jim accepted with a nod. He'd been half expecting something like this, although the when-and-where had been impossible to predict. Jim wiped a butter knife clean on his napkin and used it to cut the string tying the parcel paper together. A letter slid away from a smooth wooden box.

Baxter's handwriting was precise, each letter the perfect size. As though he were able to turn a pen into a printing press. Jim scanned the page for any error, any blot or smudge that would betray anyone trying to impersonate Baxter. To his annoyance, it was perfect. The voice rang between his ears. That would have been too easy, wouldn't it? His eyes fell to the date. January 8th, 1906. Two years ago.

Dearest Jim,

You will only be reading this letter in the event of my death. Loyal companion that you are, I knew you would not stomach eating alone at one of our usual haunts. Many times however when we would walk past this café, I made some comment or gesture toward the place so that the idea would be planted in your mind.

I decided to set plans in motion some while ago now. It became clear to me that were I no longer around to operate, the City would be sent into something of a spin.

I'm sure there is much fuss, especially from our not-so-esteemed police In-

spector. After all, how can the world's greatest analytical mind solve his own murder? As you might imagine, I find the challenge of that quite invigorating, even though I shall not be around to enjoy my own moral victory.

I presented the staff of this establishment with strict instructions on your mannerisms, your dress, and your likely order. I hope the bacon was to your liking, it was a little overdone for my tastes. However, in the event that there has been an error and my final words are to some stranger who happens to be your doppelganger—or worse, someone impersonating you for nefarious reasons—then I have locked the box. I also cannot rule out that our deaths came together, tackling some evil no doubt. In that case, I implore you, stranger, to burn this letter and leave this box to the sea. Do not give in to curiosity, do not try to open it through forced means, for it is rigged in such a way that you would suffer a nasty surprise.

If this is you Jim, and I calculate that it will be, you must solve the cipher that I have set out on the rear of the page.

Godspeed my friend.

P.S. Trust no one, not yourself. Not even me.

Not yourself. Not even me. What did that mean? Jim pushed his empty plate aside and smoothed the letter down in its place. Even in death, Baxter was still testing him. He turned the paper with great care, as though he were afraid he might shake some vital letters loose from the page.

"Waiter?"

The young man appeared briskly following his summons, making a bad job of pretending he didn't have one intrigued eye on the letter and box.

"Sir?"

"I'll need more coffee and a slice of that walnut cake. I may be here a while yet."

"Of course, Sir."

The young man scurried off to the kitchen while Jim studied the page. It was blank, to the naked untrained eye. He ran a finger over it with caution, gentle as a warm breeze on a summer's evening. The middle of the page held a different texture. Some kind of wax? His first instinct was to scratch the layer away with a knife, but he stayed his hand. He could feel Baxter still over his shoulder, raising his eyebrow in that almost insusceptible way that told Jim that was the wrong option. No. He couldn't risk damaging the page. Any corruption of the cipher would render the whole endeavour ruined. Instead, he struck a match and held it inches away from the page, far enough not to risk burning but close enough that the flicker of heat began to melt the invisible wax. Blowing out the match, he used a napkin to wipe the remainder away and lay his eyes upon the cipher.

"So, Baxter," he said with a grimace. "What do you have for me?"

KARDKJ

Jim allowed himself a moment to enjoy mastering the cipher before making his way to the bank. The bank manager, a taut man whose face indicated a sneeze would fatally rearrange his skin, allowed Jim into the vault where Baxter's box was waiting for him. He told himself to be open to anything, that any ounce of assumption would be foolish and reductive.

His assumption that he should not assume, proved to be true. Jim opened the lid which itself seemed to squeak a 'why?' as though anything Baxter had ever touched had absorbed some portion of his questioning mind.

Inside was another sealed letter, a not unsubstantial amount of money and an attached note.

Seek the aid of a friend across the sea.

Twenty years as a member of Her Majesty's armed forces had left Jim with a robust constitution when it came to sea travel, but five days traversing choppy Atlantic waters tested even his iron stomach. Still, Jim wished that it had only been his guts churning. Rest escaped him, his mind swimming with half-baked theories and annoyingly generous helpings of self-doubt. Why would Baxter want him to seek help? The answer seemed simple, but he did not want to admit it.

The smell and sounds of the city welcomed him. It was quite the relief when back on solid ground, to spy a friendly face waiting at the harbour.

"You don't look so good, Jim."

The thick Brooklyn accent hit him in the ears like a well-thrown rock. Jim hauled his case with one hand and offered a greeting with the other. "Cataneli. Impeccable as always. I'm glad to see you received my telegram."

"Yeah well. I got an image to uphold, you know? People don't trust a guy with details that can't even drag a comb through his hair."

"First impressions matter."

"That's one of his lines, right? Sorry to hear about all that. Me and him weren't exactly buddies but I respected the hell out of him. He really set a standard for guys like us. In fact, you wouldn't believe the amount of questionable women I've been able to impress just by saying we were buddies."

"But you just said—"

"They don't gotta know that."

Jim nodded. "Indeed. Do you have somewhere we can talk unbothered? I need to share something with you."

"I just moved into a new office. You can say whatever you like about whoever you like in there."

Jim fought against a wave of fatigue that tried to drag down his eyelids. The room smelled of polish and tobacco. Jim eyed a few framed photos and newspaper clippings on the wall, all hung at perfect angles. The office was organised, clean to the point of obsession. Cataneli had always kept his own appearance akin to that of a theatre star but his previous personal space had been more a collection of chaos. Loose papers and trinkets that had been collected on his various escapades. "Say, where's that ornate glass elephant you used as a paperweight?" Jim asked. "The craftsmanship on that always impressed me."

"Hm?" Cataneli paused from reading the letter and lifted his head for a moment. "Oh. That. I put a ton of stuff in storage at my folk's place in Long Island. They got a big basement. I didn't want some undesirable coming in here and smashing all my favourite stuff, you know?"

"Indeed." Jim slid a finger across the shining oak surface of the desk. "You're certainly keeping it cleaner than the last place."

"Well. I'll be damned." Cataneli looked at Jim, back to the letter and repeated the motion a few times before knocking back a shot of whiskey. "You read this?"

"I did. There's something else." Jim unfolded the rough note given to him by the Inspector and placed it atop the letter. "The Inspector gave me this. The name of the person who wanted the case solved quickly."

"Holy shit."

"I had thoughts along a similar line."

The letter contained a list of names that Baxter believed might be involved in the event of his death. One of the names appeared on both papers. Seth Low.

"So, why would the Mayor of New York want a detective from London dead?"

"We definitely ruffled a few feathers on our last visit," said Jim. "Perhaps too many feathers. Or perhaps someone with greater machinations in mind is using the mayor as a stooge."

"I know who you're thinking," said Cataneli. "Ain't no way. He's chained up eating applesauce at New York State Reformatory."

Jim eyed Cataneli. There was something slightly off about him that he couldn't place his finger on. Perhaps he'd just lost weight or combed his hair to the opposite side. The way he had ignored Jim's comment about the cleaned-up office bothered him. Baxter's warning flashed across his mind's eye. 'Trust no one.'

"Still. I think it's worth ruling out, don't you?"

"There's a few issues of a legislative nature that may be tricky to get around. Time used to be you could slip the governor fifty dollars and get an audience with whomever the hell you wanted. But times have changed. You want to visit someone that notorious, you're gonna need to grease a bigger wheel than that."

"Who?" Asked Jim, already realising the answer as the vowel left his lips.

Cataneli pushed the letter and scrap of paper back toward him. "Take one guess."

Jim tossed and turned. Baxter had left enough money for a hotel room that offered every physical comfort imaginable. However, soft sheets and plump pillows were no answer to the questions plaguing his mind.

Hoping to find comfort in the warming aromas of his pipe, Jim rose from the bed and lit the lamp standing proudly dust-free on the bedside table.

Whistling in a pattern that he could not place or get out of his head as he packed tobacco down into the pipe, a noise from beyond the curtains caught his attention. Not willing to share his pipe with a stray cat or pigeon out on the balcony, Jim paused for a moment. Instinct told him to reach for his revolver as something tried to turn the handle from the outside. Not a stray cat.

"I'm armed," Jim called, raising his weapon. "And I will shoot. Identify yourself."

"Jim? Is that you?" A muffled voice—familiar, yet not as familiar as it should have been—called from outside.

Jim drew the thick curtains open with caution, pulling to the side but keeping the revolver trained on the doors. On seeing the uninvited guest, Jim unlocked the doors.

Peter Cataneli stood on the balcony, gun in hand.

"What on earth are you doing, man?"

"I got a tip-off saying Baxter's killer was in this room," he said. "What are you doing? Why didn't you tell me you were in town?"

"We were together a few hours ago." Jim's mind raced as a picture began to form. Cataneli stepped inside, somehow having lost an inch in height and gaining about six on his shoulders. "Tell me, do you still have the glass elephant?"

"Sure, I do. What you got in that pipe? I ain't seen you for two years."

Jim shook his head, hoping to throw off the ridiculous notions trying to settle there. A word, beginning with the letter 'I' tried to push itself to the forefront of his mind but a Baxter-shaped lock refused it entry.

"Clearly, we have both been lead amiss," he managed. "As far as I was aware, you met me on the docks and then took me to your new office."

"New office? Man, I can barely afford the rent on my current one. What the hell is going—"

The sound of a gunshot whip-cracked through the air. Peter fell forward with the breath caught in his lungs. Behind them, an empty glass vase shattered. Jim cushioned him to the floor as a blood-red flower bloomed through the fabric of his grey coat.

"Son of a bitch!" Cataneli grimaced.

"Easy old boy," Jim said. He pulled a blue handkerchief from the breast pocket of his pyjamas. It was a practice Baxter had always sneered at, but Jim had held firm the notion that a gentleman should remain so even in slumber. With gentle yet urgent care earned through years of dressing field wounds, he pulled back Cataneli's coat and shirt, pressing the handkerchief firmly against the wound.

"As the glass on the carpet can attest to, the bullet passed clean through which is good on two counts. One, it means I won't have to dig around in your shoulder and risk infection removing the bullet. Secondly, it gives us a better chance at identifying the projectile and perhaps even the shooter."

Cataneli eased himself up on the hotel bed, his shoulder now stitched and bandaged. "I don't know what I'm more grateful for Jim, your emergency field kit or your emergency Scotch."

Jim raised a smile. "I never travel without either. Besides, the whiskey has multiple uses, both as an anaesthetic and as pain relief."

Having rescued the bullet from the shards of glass, he held it up to the lamp with a pair of tweezers, eye pressed to his magnifying glass.

"Hmm. If I know my rifles and I believe that I do, this fellow was fired from a Winchester 1894. The question is, did our assailant mistake you for a deer who had someone found himself on the fifth-floor balcony, or more likely, did he facilitate you being here?"

"Christ." Cataneli drained his glass and grimaced as he lowered his arm. "So we got someone running around pretending to be me who then decides he wants the real me out of the picture?"

"I don't think so," said Jim. "The shot was perfectly placed. Why, it barely nicked a blood vessel. It takes either a shot of the utmost luck or someone with the rare combination of a deadly eye and explicit knowledge of the internal mappings of the human body."

"So why shoot me then?"

"I don't know. A test. A game."

Jim placed the bullet down and rubbed at his temples. None of this made sense. How could a man wear the face of another so convincingly?

Jim went through the letter and the Inspector's note with the real Cataneli.

"I don't buy it," he said. "I'd have heard if the mayor was dirty. That kind of thing travels the streets like syphilis."

"So someone is using him as a patsy then, as I suggested to the other you."

"You said this doppelganger was trying to put you off visiting our most famous incarcerated resident. Why do you think that is?"

Jim shuffled ideas and theories in his mind's eye like a deck of cards, except every reveal was a joker.

Cards. A calling card. What a fool! Jim returned an examining eye to the bullet, turning it over and over in all directions until he made out the mark. There it was. Initials, marked into the bullet with an incredibly steady hand. The kind of hand that could shoot a man with barely any damage in the dark from a rooftop away. The obvious stared him in the face until he could refuse it no longer.

"You planning on filling me in there, Jim?"

Jim let a heavy, chest-deflating sigh escape his lips. "I had thought, perhaps foolishly, that he had played no part in this. For how could I ever hoped to get the best of the man who was Baxter's equal, in every measure? Yet it is clear to me now, old friend. We must find a way of speaking with John Doyle."

Much like an actor and the play that could not be named, Jim hesitated to even speak the man's name aloud. John Doyle possessed all of Baxter's grand intelligence, all of his hubris, and not a jot of his desire to use any of those gifts to help anyone but himself. Yet, Doyle had only ever been interested in sparring with Baxter. Jim had often suspected that Doyle had barely been aware of his presence, no matter how large a part he had played in helping to avert any one of his nefarious schemes. Perhaps there had been a miscalculation in the machinations of Doyle, and Jim was just a loose end to be tied up. If so, why go to all these efforts to punish him? Jim was acutely aware of missing several pieces of the puzzle.

The following morning, he spent a short time speaking to the hotel manager and a few other guests to garner if anyone had caught sight of the shooter. Not only had he not been spotted, it turned out the shot had not been heard. Frustration burned like a white-hot brand of failure in his mind.

After a rushed breakfast, Jim and Cataneli went to pay a visit to the office that Jim had unwittingly attended only the day before. As he expected but not as he hoped, it was abandoned and empty. Again, attempted information from the surrounding offices and apartments was fruitless. It was as though a ghost was several steps ahead of him.

Jim sat alone in a small coffee house, staring at an empty cup and puffing on his pipe with an air of resignation. Someone had roughly carved '6th Street Boys' into the soft wood of the table. The words he last spoke to Adelaide echoed with mocking intent between his ears. What a fool he had been. Not only was he no closer to catching the killer, but he had been caught up in a game of which he had no concept of the rules. Cataneli. The real one—or was he? A chill found the freedom of his spine. What if *this* Cataneli was the fraud? Or another fraud? Damn it. He had enough red herrings to feed a village of Vikings. Pull yourself together man. Baxter's words attacked his self-pitying stupor. *You've missed something. Some detail that you took in when you didn't even realise you were looking.*

Whomever this Cataneli was had left ten minutes prior, to send a telegram to a friend at The New York World newspaper, who might be able to put him in touch with the Governor of New York State Reformatory. The same Cataneli, as far as he could tell, returned brandishing a newspaper bearing the same name. Jim felt a sense of relief as Cataneli held the item on his uninjured side.

"I didn't make it to the telegram office, didn't need to. Got an earful from a newsie. Take a look at this."

Jim lifted the paper and held it out a few inches from his nose. The bold headline ripped another clue away and set fire to it.

CRIMINAL MASTERMIND DOYLE FOUND HANGED IN CELL

Jim crumpled the paper in one fist and threw it across the table.

"Hey, that cost me two cents!" Cataneli said. "And more than that, you should read the article. Especially the part where Doyle leaves a suicide note saying how he don't wanna live in a world without 'the only mind capable of stimulating his.' Got a whole 'and he wept as there were no more worlds to conquer' kind of vibe."

Jim stubbed out his pipe. "Do you have any doubt as to the authenticity of this?"

"I don't think so. It's running on every paper in the city, the streets are buzzing with the news. It's too big to be a fake."

"It appears I have been pulling at another empty thread. Damn it!" Jim slammed a fist down onto the table, causing his empty cup to jump up.

"Take it easy. Where's that British gentlemanly conduct I'm always hearing about?"

"My apologies," said Jim. "I fear I have been sent on a wild goose chase and dragged you along for the ride."

"Well, I ain't got nowhere else to be. I'm real eager on finding out who's got the nerve to run around pretending to be me. Besides, just 'cus Doyle's bought himself a one-way ticket to eternal damnation, doesn't mean he isn't involved."

"No," said Jim. "Doyle needs his ego stroked. If this was truly him, he'd want credit. There is no way he would put all of these moving parts into place without some grand reveal. I dare say this about a dead man—even him. But his suicide may be the first fly in the ointment of whoever is ultimately behind all of this."

"So, we're back to who."

"And why." Jim tapped his empty pipe on the corner of the table. "The why will lead us to the who."

He continued to tap his pipe, in a rhythm both strangely familiar and yet of which he could not quite name.

"Whatever new nemesis this is, knew us both well enough to somehow convincingly pass off as you and knew that I would be here. Someone so skilled that they could carve a dead man's initials into a bullet." Oh God. Jim felt hot bile gather in the base of his throat. "The letter. The money. It had been so convincingly written in Baxter's word and tone that I had not taken a moment to doubt it." A foolish error borne of emotion, ego, and desperation. He wanted it to be true. He wanted to believe that Baxter saw him as an equal, capable of solving the greatest of crimes. "This whole thing had been a ruse, clearly. But to what end?"

"I get it," said Cataneli. "My head's spinning too. Want my opinion?"

"I welcome it."

"This is personal. Not to Baxter, but to you. Whoever is pulling all these strings was never after Baxter. They got a grudge against you. They want to grind you down and make you doubt yourself. Maybe they took out Baxter first because they knew they'd have to get past him to get to you. So you gotta ask, who knows you? Who knows about your past? And maybe most important—who would they go after next?"

Jim thought on Cataneli's words, staring down into the vacant coffee cup. No villain or foe truly cared about him, surely. It was only ever Baxter. Still, there was something in the advice that loosened a screw somewhere. A picture began to form in his mind, clues that he didn't realise were clues coalesced until they formed a shape, a figure he was both familiar with but feared he would never be close to again.

"I do believe you may be on to something, or half onto something I should say. Not a grudge as such, but a lover. Spurned by circumstance and by duty. A person of talent and resources able to move the pieces around the board."

"You don't mean?"

"I'm afraid I do, and it breaks my heart to say it. I do believe the person behind all of this can be no other than Adelaide Harmen."

"I dunno," Cataneli said with a shake of the head for emphasis. "She loves you. Any fool can see that."

"And yet she fears I love my commitment to duty more. Think about it. She trained as an actress, she has the wealth and influence to whisper in the ears of politicians and royals. Often did she tell me fond tales of her youth where her father would take her hunting. I did not see it before now because I did not want to entertain the thought. She blamed her brother for us not being together. Cleary, the resentment grew to intolerable levels."

Cataneli pulled a dented old cigarette case from his good side and tapped out a cigarette. "What will you do now?" he asked, cigarette hanging unlit on his lip.

"I must return home, although god knows how I go about this."

The idea of confronting Adelaide, of calling her a murderer, made him sick to his stomach.

"Well," said Cataneli as he lit the cigarette, before shaking the flame from the match. "In my experience working alongside the law but sometimes having to get around it, you gotta make your own evidence."

"I'm afraid I don't follow."

Jim's mind was covered in a fog more dense than the worst day in London had to offer. He couldn't think, couldn't see ahead. Only a vague shape in the form of Adelaide.

"I got a theory. But first I got to ask you a couple of questions."

"Have at it." Jim waved a weary hand.

"One, where'd you get that funny-smelling tobacco?"

The tobacco. Jim had been smoking it ever since Baxter had died.

"It was Baxter's, I found an amount in his study. This may sound foolish but I thought perhaps smoking what he smoked might bring me some of the same clarity." What Jim couldn't admit was that it had also brought him a comfort he had come to rely on.

"Huh." Cataneli took a deep draw on his cigarette before tapping out a small pile of ash in the well-used ashtray in the centre of the table. "I thought it smelled familiar. Do you remember?"

Jim wanted to see whatever answer Cataneli was angling at, but he could not. The sense of his own failure bit at him. A cruel, gnawing pain. He wanted to be wrong about Adelaide, but there seemed no other answer. Sadness seeped into every fibre of him, as though it were being poured into his soul.

"I'm afraid I do not. I cannot see past Adelaide."

"Ten years ago," said Cataneli, "when I was still a little wet behind the ears. I was in awe of Baxter, the famous 'world's greatest detective.' I followed you guys everywhere like a damn puppy."

Jim welcomed the memory, anything to distract him from the emotional weight dragging him down. The case of the Mind Master.

"Of course. Baxter was constantly annoyed by your presence, as I remember. Although I do believe he developed some respect for your enthusiasm for learning."

"Well he had a funny way of showing it. Anyway, that guy behind all those missing museum pieces, who claimed he could control people's minds. Remember what we found in his shisha pipe?"

"He claimed that was how he was gaining access to so many riches without a fight," said Jim slowly as the memory rolled out in his mind's eye. "People would simply hand over whatever he asked them for."

"Right. That damn smell has stuck with me. I knew it was familiar."

Realisation crept up on Jim like a long shadow during sunset. The power of suggestion. The Mind Master had claimed to be a disciple of some Far Eastern shaman, gaining supernatural abilities.

"But it was all nonsense. Smoke and mirrors. The tobacco was just mixed with fragrant spices"

"What if it wasn't?"

Through his confusion and exhaustion, Jim saw a twinkle in Cataneli's eye, which brought a welcome shot of hope to his anxious heart. "Are you saying that whoever is behind all of this planted some 'magic' herb in Baxter's study for me to find, to make me pliable?"

"I think maybe someone wanted to lead you down a certain path," said Cataneli. "Make you doubt yourself and make you see what they wanted you to see. And from what you've told me, I just don't see Adelaide doing that."

The notion that someone had been pulling strings, moving him around a board, lit a furious fire within him. He so badly wanted it to be not Adelaide that he couldn't tell if his heart was filling his head with false hope.

"If not her, then who?"

"Someone with an ego to rival Doyle, or Baxter. Someone who, at some point, will want credit for taking both of them off the board."

Finally, Jim's head began to clear. All this time he had been operating on the assumption that he needed to be like Baxter, to emulate him. Now he saw what a futile exercise that had been. There were no rules to play by. So much detail surrounding Baxter's death refused to follow any logical path. He couldn't solve this by pondering on what Baxter would have done.

"We need to find a way to draw them out. But how?"

Cataneli lit another cigarette. "We provide some evidence, set someone up to take the blame. That person just needs to play the role the right way."

Jim caught the way Cataneli was looking at him and knew where this was going. He'd have to lie to Mrs Walmley, and to Adelaide. He'd have to make everyone believe the very worst in him.

"It would seem that there is no other way. Let us end this."

Jim awoke in his own bed for the first time in almost a month. The crossing back home had been mercifully more gentle, yet he had known what was waiting for him would be anything but. They had everything in place. A letter had been sent, an item had been left in a place, waiting to be found.

Jim faced the thought that this might be the final time he'd ever sleep in this room if their plan failed. Exhaustion and stress pulled him into a deep sleep, eventually interrupted by the scolding mutterings of Mrs. Walmley.

He left his room, feet in slippers and his robe wrapped around him. Mrs Walmley attacked what appeared to be a stubborn, yet invisible, cobweb with a duster.

"Is everything all right?" Jim asked.

"You know me, Mr Whitmore. I don't intrude in the business of others."

Jim couldn't but help but stifle a smile, yet it was tempered by knowing what he had to do.

"Of course not," he said. "Forgive me, perhaps it is the after-effects of long travel. But I can't shake the feeling that I have somehow left you with an annoyance that I do not know the cause of."

Mrs Walmley continued with her diligence, to the point where Jim began to feel sorry for the wall lamp in its robust encounter with the duster. She continued with her attack, before managing a shake of the head and a large sigh.

"Miss Adelaide stopped by yesterday afternoon. Floods of tears, she was. She showed me the letter you left for her. I always thought of you as a brave, kind soul. But that letter. Well forgive me, but that letter was cold and cruel."

Jim took a moment. He had not looked forward to this, but he had no choice. He had to play the part, had to become someone capable of such lies in all of their eyes.

"I sent no such letter, Mrs Walmley."

"She said you accused her of murdering her brother!"

Jim appeared faint, leaning against the bedroom doorway for support. "I did no such thing, I promise you. And yet…"

Damn it. The urge to tell her the truth was almost too strong, yet he knew that he could not.

"Mrs Walmley, I do believe that years of grief and resentment have warped

Adelaide's mind. Although I did not yet accuse her, I'm afraid I have drawn the conclusion that she is in fact, behind her brother's death."

"I'm sorry, Mr Whitmore. She said the Inspector had been in touch. They found new evidence. They know that…"

Mrs. Walmley didn't need to finish her sentence as downstairs, heavy hands knocked on the front door. He heard the police call his name. Jim drew a deep breath. There was no escape now, no turning back. He had to trust in himself, and in Cataneli.

"Mrs Walmley…Joan. Please. I swear I did not do this. I swear it on the grave of my late wife. I did not kill Baxter."

She turned away from him, tears in her eyes.

"I don't know what to believe anymore," she said in a small, quiet voice.

Jim woke in a dark prison cell, his head bruised. The arresting sergeant had seen fit to strike him, even though Jim did not fight being taken into custody.

Slits of light daggered in through a narrow window. Jim rubbed at the sore skin on his wrists where he had been cuffed. It was difficult to tell how long he had been in here already. He had been served no food, and only a foggy half-memory of a cup of water indicated some passage of time.

"I should have known," said the Inspector, approaching the bars of the cell. "You made it obvious, really. You said that you should be a suspect. Were you mocking us?"

"Someone is mocking the both of us," Jim said with a croak, his lips cracked and throat dry. "I believed it to be Adelaide, but now I am not so sure. I'm not sure of anything, apart from the quite vital fact that I am an innocent man."

"We had several new witnesses come forward, telling us that you were seen confronting Baxter in a drunken rage, the night of his death. Some disgusting back-alley opium den. You were angry that he would not let you marry his sister. You took advantage of his inebriated state, followed him home, and took his life."

"No," Jim tried to shake away the lies. "No, this is preposterous! This is not the truth; this is not what Baxter wanted!"

As absurd as it was, he couldn't help but wonder what Adelaide would make of his acting. He held on to the hope that one day, he would get to tell her everything.

"Jim, we found a blue, bloodied handkerchief stashed behind a bush near the murder scene. It's the type you always carry."

"No, you don't understand. We're all pawns in the game of some new master. Whoever dressed as Peter Cataneli in New York must have broken into my hotel room, got an earlier ship back here. Don't you see?"

"I take no pleasure in this," The inspector spoke with what appeared to be a genuine sadness. "You're not making any sense, Jim. It sounds like the ramblings of a…"

"A madman? Is that what you think I have become?"

"A disturbed mind."

"No," Jim said. "No! You don't understand. I have to catch them. I have to do my duty. Send a telegram to Mr. Peter Cataneli of New York. He can tell you. He can corroborate everything."

The Inspector turned away. "You're to be killed by firing squad. It is decided. Come clean, Jim. You're going to die. At least die an honest man."

The words caught in his throat, yet he knew he would have to release them. There was no other way, as painful as it was.

"Fine. I confess. I did it. Let it be known that I, Jim Whitmore killed Baxter Harmen. I murdered that smug bastard. He thought he was so much better than me. And yet, here we are."

The words sounded so strange, even knowing they were in service of what he hoped would finally be the truth. Despite that, Jim felt some sense of relief at being able to speak about Baxter in such a way. Had he been denying those feelings for all those years? Focus on the task at hand, he told himself. He took a calming breath, sat down against the wall and closed his eyes.

Jim drifted in and out of restless sleep, haunted by dreams of Baxter.

"On your feet, Whitmore."

A gruff, low voice jangled keys. Jim's eyes adjusted as a lit lamp burnt a hole in the darkness.

"Is it time?" he asked. "Is this the end?"

"You're being moved. Order from the Home Secretary. You've caused quite the stir, Jim. Murdering the great hero Baxter Harmen. I'm surprised the prison hasn't been breached by a pitchfork-wielding mob already."

The officer, his face shrouded in shadow, tossed Jim a small yet thick woollen sack.

"Place this over your head and then put your hands out."

Jim obliged, struggling to breathe as the itchy wool tickled his nose. He felt hard cold metal cuffs pressed against his outstretched wrists before he was wrenched to his feet by the collar. He tried to count the steps and turns as he was dragged along, but in his exhausted state it was difficult to keep track. After a few minutes of doors and corridors, he felt the wind on his back and grass and gravel under his feet. After days? A week? Inside the damp dark cell, it was a relief to be outside, even in his current predicament.

"Stop. On your knees."

The gruff voice had barely said a word since they had left the cell apart from the odd direction. Jim knelt down and braced himself, he had a good sense of what was coming next. Something hard and heavy smacked into the back of his head and he crumpled to the floor.

Jim opened his eyes. He was relieved to take a deep breath free of the mask, even though the back of his head throbbed in resistance to his sudden consciousness. He was also in far more comforting surroundings than he had been previously. Although he was now cuffed around a bedpost, the bed itself was well made up and a soothing comfort to his sore back. Pink and gold splashes of dawn made symmetrical patterns on the wall through pristine net curtains hanging in the window. In one corner was a full-length mirror. In the other, hiding in an armchair and still mostly untouched by light, sat a tall, thin man in a police uniform. Jim allowed himself a moment of satisfaction. He still didn't have the who, but it appeared as though Cataneli's instinct had been correct. They'd managed to prick the ego of whatever madman was behind all of this.

"I wasn't aware The Tower of London had a first-class suite," said Jim. "Is there a breakfast menu I could peruse? I could quite go for a smoked kipper and a piping hot pot of tea."

"Quiet."

"Or what?" Jim sat up as bed he could, squinting at his new captor. "Rather hard to threaten a man about to die. I don't know if you heard, but I killed the amazing Baxter Harmen."

The man in the chair did not respond at first, but Jim spotted a brief clenching of the jaw.

"It was easier than I expected, too," Jim pressed. "No Machiavellian scheming required."

"I said quiet."

The fingernails were digging into the armchair now. The light, now filling the room began to roll over him. Only his face remained truly out of sight.

"I don't think I shall waste my final moments in silence," said Jim. "No, I do believe that I should enjoy my victory. Tell me, what are they saying in the press, in the streets? I bet I even have supporters. A lot of people didn't like him, you know. They called him aloof. A freak, even. Nothing more than another circus curiosity."

The man stood now, silent rage emanating from him.

"No. The masses adored him. They needed him. Whereas *you*." The man spat the word with venom. "No one will mourn you. No one will remember your name."

"You're wrong," said Jim. "I had a beloved. And friends. I know my value, far too late, but I know my worth as a man. And it is not to be the put-upon sidekick of some arrogant fool with a magnifying glass and a messiah complex."

Jim felt his chest heave up and down, hot breath fuelled by indignant rage. Just like in the prison, there was a freedom in talking about Baxter in such a way. Was it even an act anymore?

"I'll show them. I'll show them that they need me."

"Me?" Jim stuttered. The possible identity of the man before him was boring into his mind. Why else would they be so defensive about Baxter?

No. It couldn't be.

"Someone will have to take his place. I...I studied him. I know his ways."

"Arrogant was being kind," said Jim. "Now show me your face, you coward."

"You do not make demands of me." The voice was slipping. The deep, throaty tone becoming something much more familiar.

Jim felt a wave of anger fill him as he pulled with all his might against the bedpost. Was this how Samson had felt? So many mixed feelings. The betrayal. The heartbreak. The chance to enact one final justice.

"Show me your face. You simpleton!"

That did it. The man stepped forward into the light.

"Simpleton?" he hissed. "You stupid, uneducated brute. You're a blunt instrument, a tool I used when I needed it. How dare you. You are nothing."

Jim couldn't help the laugh that tumbled from him. He didn't recognise most of the features. The nose was long and pointed, the chin dimpled. But there was no hiding the self-important ferocity in those eyes. Realism rushed in. Of course there was only one person who possibly could have planned all of this. A man with a hatred for the word had managed to carry out the impossible. Jim couldn't believe what he was about to say, but the truth was staring him right in the face.

"Hello, Baxter. You're looking well for a dead man."

Baxter paused, fixing Jim with a stare that sent a shudder down his spine. It was beyond cold, it was inhuman.

"What do you have to say for yourself?" Jim asked.

"Oh, Jim. Dear, simple Jim."

To Jim's surprise, Baxter fell into a relaxed state. The rigid posture of his imaginary police officer evaporated, and his shoulders folded down. He sat at the end of the bed, removing his prosthetic facial appendages.

The adrenaline surge that had carried Jim through the reunion faded. Exhaustion gripped him.

"Why?"

"Always a pertinent question, albeit one you began asking far too late. Honestly, I'm disappointed. I didn't think it would take you this long. I could say I'm insulted. Me, bested by some common criminal in an alleyway?"

"I read the coroner's report," said Jim. "Do you think I wanted to believe it? I did what you taught me. I believed the facts."

"I also told you to trust no one. Even me. I wrote it in ink and still you did not see it. I'm afraid you proved my thesis correct."

"What thesis?"

Baxter stood and turned his back, hands at his side. The anger fought its way back. *He doesn't even think you're worth addressing directly.*

"For all my intellect, I began to wonder. What if I became the victim of gross misfortune? A stray bullet. Disease. Some other incident. I knew there was no one worthy to take my place. It became my grandest game, how to solve my own murder. I wondered if I could still pull your strings from beyond the grave. It was all too easy. I studied disciplines beyond your understanding, mastering them all. I studied the greatest spies and assassins throughout history. All men and women who claim to possess some otherworldly magic or another. I can become anyone, and blend into any situation. Had I the urge, I could walk into Buckingham Palace tomorrow as the King and his own family would not be able to tell the difference. Becoming a buffoon such as Cataneli? Child's play. I see now why you two always got along so well. You're fortunate I showed him mercy. I gave you clue after clue, and you fought the obvious at every step. Between that? A few simple letters. Paying whatever scum wanted the role a pittance to take the blame for my 'murder.' They at least had the sense to remain anonymous."

Even after everything, Jim found it difficult to digest what he was hearing.

Yet, he knew he was close. He had to follow along the path they'd started on.

"You didn't foresee this though, did you? You didn't think I'd take the blame for your murder."

"No," Baxter replied with an eerie calm. "I did not believe even you to be so careless. As I said, I am disappointed."

"Did you facilitate my escape to spare my life through some vestige of friend-ship, or could you not bear the thought of the public believing I'd bested you?"

Jim knew the answer, he just had to keep him talking as he strained against the handcuffs.

"A course I can easily correct. I manipulated that ridiculous inspector once. I can do it again."

"You didn't answer my question." Jim felt the conflict. Did he want to believe that Baxter had saved him for a reason, even if he'd never admit it?

"Nor shall I. I suppose the question is, what now? Clearly, identity is no lon-ger an issue. I can be whomever I need to be. As for you? Well, you need a refresher in Morse code, at the very least."

"Are you operating under the impression that we return to some twisted status quo?" Jim laughed. "Arrogant and deluded."

"What else will you do?"

That was it. The last bit of fuel he needed. Jim pushed, and the bedpost fell apart with a crack. Baxter turned at the noise. Jim lunged at him, aiming to wrap the chains of the handcuffs around his neck. With dismissive ease, Baxter sidestepped and brought a fist crashing into Jim's nose with a wet pop. Jim fell to the floor, blood gushing into his mouth.

"Jim." Baxter knelt, eyeing Jim with curiosity. "Why do you continue to dis-appoint me?"

Jim struggled to his knees, his head spinning. "I was too close," he said. "I couldn't see it. But my friend did. I know Morse code, and it spelled out an address. This address." Jim could hear the rush of bodies enter the room as he failed to keep his eyes open.

He could hear his name being called, muffled as though he were sinking below water. He was aware of someone pulling him to his feet. Forcing himself to focus, he looked at Cataneli holding him up.

"Thank you."

"Holy shit," said Cataneli.

"My thoughts exactly," Jim said weakly.

A group of police officers had Baxter handcuffed, and the Inspector stood in front of him.

"You," Baxter sneered. "You buffoon. What's your plan now? Arrest a dead man?"

"I should have known," said The Inspector. "Even 'dead' you were bound to cause me trouble. I'm not sure you deserve to be arrested."

The Inspector pulled a revolver from his hip and held it out to Jim. "I believe this belongs to you?"

Jim took a breath, wiped blood from his face and took the weapon. He thought of the lies and counter-lies that had got them all to this point. He raised the gun, aiming at Baxter's forehead. Could he do this? Even after everything, could he truly kill Baxter? The bastard deserved no mercy, he knew that, however thoughts of Adelaide stayed his hand.

"There can be no worse fate," Baxter said, "than the world knowing that I was bested by the likes of *you.*"

Jim moved his revolver to the side, thumb sliding away from the hammer with reluctance.

"I can think of one," he said. "Gentleman, we've all been chasing a lie for the last month. Here we are at the end, and our solution is another lie. I dare say this is one of many outcomes that Baxter would have calculated as a possibility. However, I do believe that there is a fate worse for him that we should consider."

"And what would that be, Jim? Do you plan to moralise me into unconsciousness?"

"No," Jim said. "While I must apologise to the Inspector for the mountains

of inconvenient paperwork coming his way, I do believe that there is one simple solution."

"You sure about this, Jim?" Cataneli stood by his side, shoulder to shoulder.

Jim nodded with solemn certainty. The world deserved the truth. Adelaide
deserved the truth, no matter how painful. He could only hope that she could still love
him through the outcome that he was about to propose.

"Let us tell the truth. Every headline across the world. Every conversation in
every restaurant, every pub. Schoolground gossip. They will mock you; they will turn
on you. And in the end, all they will remember is a man who got caught by his own
hubris."

"You will be nothing without me. You will have no worth."

Jim thought once more of Adelaide. Of quiet walks on Sunday afternoons. He
thought of laughter, the joyful spontaneous bursts that only made sense to two souls
intertwined and how his heart pined for her every moment that they were apart, and on
what a fool he had been to ever put duty before love.

"On the contrary, Baxter. Without you, I will have everything."

10/14/85

I am writing to you from the tubular past to check your progress in solving our little game. While you're having a bangin' time reading these stories, I totally performed a date shift by hopping a DeLorean to the decade of neon, synthpop, and excess.

Time is weird, isn't it? Even writing that date at the top made me feel like, whoa. Everything exists all at once and the only thing that's real right now is the moment you're living in. Totally non-heinous.

I can't speak for like, the whole universe or whatever, but sometimes, everything really is connected and there are no accidents. Remember that, and you'll be clutch. If you do get stuck though, don't wig out. Take a chill pill and check the hints in the back for a little nudge in the right direction.

The future calls. I gotta motor.

Stay legit,
Amanda

REMEMBER THAT TIME WE SAVED THE WORLD?

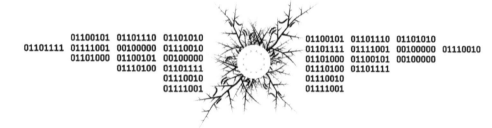

01100101 01101110 01101010
01101111 01111001 00100000 01110010
01101000 01100101 00100000
01110100 01101111
01110010
01111001

01100101 01101110 01101010
01101111 01111001 00100000 01110010
01101000 01100101 00100000
01110100 01101111
01110010
01111001

BY KYLE A. MASSA

The Prologue

A prologue is a dreadful way to start a story. That's why we're skipping it.

The Prophecy

Let's begin here instead. The Prophecy comes from the Witch, and it goes like this:

"From 'neath his grave he'll rise again,

from one of nine he'll come,

the first person shall triumph then,

and all days shall be done."

Got it? Good. Now let's discuss our setting.

The Setting

The Witch's manor is a weathered building, all creaking and moldy, its paint peeling, its gardens wilting, its shades drawn like the eyes of a sleeper. Stone gargoyles crouch atop the roof, and though they once had faces, they've been worn featureless by time.

Inside, the halls smell of mildew and must and flowers long gone to rot. The paintings on the walls leer behind veils of dust, their unblinking eyes following visitors, though visitors are rare enough. There are many rooms, both up the spiral stairs and down, yet few are ever used. Pay closest attention to the library, four floors up and five doors down, on your left. That's where we'll be spending most of our story.

Only two souls call this manor home: The first is the aforementioned Witch, while the second is her servant, a man whose name is immaterial to this story. That's Witch with a capital W, yes, and yes, she's the same Witch you read about in your books when you were young. She's the Witch most famous for being one of nine, nine who deposed the Dark Lord.

Of course you know that story. We all do.

The Witch awaits in her library, hunched beneath a blanket at the head of a long table, a fire crackling in the hearth beside her. Her guests will be arriving shortly.

What guests, you ask? It's the nine who defied the Dark Lord forty years ago—or those of them who remain. In no particular order, they are the Merchant, the Barbarian, the King, and the Ranger. You've heard of them all, for they all saved the Realm and brought everlasting peace. But now, in this story, perhaps for the first time, you shall meet them.

Watch as they approach the Witch's manor.

The Merchant's Approach

The Merchant arrives alone, as requested in the Witch's invitation. She's unaccustomed to such an arrangement, for she always rides in a lavish carriage pulled by several sturdy horses, steered by a coachman whose annual income contains many zeros. Not so tonight, but at least her mount is capable: a fleet-footed thoroughbred with a coat as black as the surrounding gloom.

She halts before the manor and dismounts, her clothes jingling with every move. To her horse, she says, "Ever been to a reunion with coworkers you didn't always like and haven't seen in forty years?" Then, thinking better of it, she adds, "You know what? Don't answer that."

The Barbarian's Approach

The Barbarian rides alone as well, though his mount is far less expensive than the Merchant's. Unlike the Merchant, he doesn't have numbers on the mind. Instead, it's words.

At this point in his life, now four decades removed from the death of the Dark Lord, he'd rather be known as the Playwright than the Barbarian. He's not the buff, shirtless, swaggering adventurer he once was, after all. He's cultured now. Articulate. He's taken several lessons in playwriting since their quest, and he's written many scripts.

And have any of them seen the stage? No, not a single one. But don't mention that to the Barbarian—he's sensitive.

"What's a good rhyme for 'bacon?'" he asks aloud.

The King's Approach

The King is unaccustomed to being alone like this. There are always people fussing over him. Still, now that he's slipped them for the time being, the solitude isn't altogether unpleasant. It reminds him of his exiled days, when he dueled ruffians and slayed monsters and courted wenches (they never liked when he called them wenches). Though decades have passed since those days, he still looks as handsome now as he did then, what with his broad smile and his luscious locks.

He dismounts from his horse and runs his fingers through his hair, and when he glances into his palm, he finds something alarming: several loose strands. He holds one up to the meager moonlight.

"Is that…a gray?" he whispers in horror. He casts it aside like it's incriminating evidence.

The Ranger's Approach

Unlike the others, the Ranger doesn't arrive on horseback. She travels the same way she always has: alone, and on foot. Bare feet, that is, soles blackened by the road and turned hard as leather. She carries her longbow over one shoulder, along with a small bag packed with essentials.

She stops. Listens. Hears something. She whips around, bow drawn, arrow nocked, she aims, pulls, fires, and—

Misses. Her arrow goes sailing off into the gloom. The animal she'd been aiming at stands motionless for a moment, then scurries away.

"Fucking squirrels," the Ranger grumbles. Then she heads toward the manor.

Their Arrival

The Ranger arrives first, because she travels lightest and swiftest of them all. The Merchant arrives shortly after, because she values punctuality. Third comes the Barbarian, because he was struck by sudden inspiration and had to write it down. Then, lastly, the King, because he believes a King should always arrive last, just to show everyone whose time is most important.

The Witch's unnamed servant greets each guest at the door, then shows them to the library to reunite with their host. She awaits at the head of the table, and once her guests are seated, we resume our story where it began, with the prophecy, which the Witch delivers like so…

"From 'neath his grave he'll rise again,

from one of nine he'll come,

the first person shall triumph then,

and all days shall be done."

"There," the Witch finishes. "Now if you'll excuse me…"

She keels over face down on the table with a heavy thud. She says nothing more.

The Subsequent Conversation

An awkward silence follows.

"Umm." The King pokes the Witch. "Shall I call for some coffee?"

"I don't think she's asleep," the Merchant murmurs.

The Barbarian shudders. "With her last words, she warns us. This must be why she summoned us—one final prophecy before her death. Our Witch. Our dear Witch."

"Our dear *dead* Witch, you mean," the Merchant breathes. "Don't touch anything. No food, no water. This looks like poison's work."

The Ranger stares, but says nothing.

The King stands, crouches next to the Witch's slumped figure, and pokes her. "Wakey wakey."

She doesn't wakey. She would've slid off her chair if the King hadn't caught her. He sets her back in her seat and sighs. "Alas. She's dead."

"'From one of nine he'll come,'" the Barbarian quotes. "What do we make of that?"

The Merchant scans the shadowy room. "What does it matter? She's gone, as our great liege informed us. I'm a tad more interested in how she managed to die so suddenly."

"But she's our friend!" the Barbarian protests.

"Subject," the King corrects.

"Business associate," the Merchant clarifies.

And still the Ranger says nothing.

The Barbarian shakes his head. "You're all uncivilized. If you won't mourn, at least remember. Four decades ago, during our quest together, the Witch's prophecies always came true. Every one of them."

"How could we forget?" The King strikes an especially kingly pose. Then, patting the corpse of the Witch on the shoulder, he eases back into his chair. "Some reunion this has been. We're here for five minutes and our host dies on us. I expect this means there won't be refreshments."

"Someone should tell her servant," says the Barbarian. "It should be delicately done, and since you three have proven to be so callous…" He rises, strides across the room, and reaches for the door.

There is a rustle of fabric, the twang of a string, and a thunk as an arrow sprouts from the door, perhaps an inch above the Barbarian's outstretched fingers.

"That's my writing hand," the Barbarian whispers in horror.

"I know. I missed." The Ranger pulls a second arrow from her quiver and loads it. "You're not leaving. No one is. Not until we find the Dark Lord's minion."

A moment of quiet follows, filled only by the crackle of the fire, its shadows flickering wildly over the walls.

"Wait." The King makes a sour face. "Who said anything about the Dark Lord?"

"Who else could rise from his grave? Who else can bring the end of days? The Witch's prophecy means one of us here, today, shall resurrect him. Or perhaps give birth to him—I'm not sure which."

The King's expression turns from sour to incredulous. He forces several guffaws. "Ranger, you were always strange. But I never took you for irrational."

"Perhaps not." The Barbarian stalks back to the table and slumps into his seat. "Reluctant as I am to defend someone who just shot at me, I believe our Ranger might have a point. The Witch's prophecies were never wrong."

The Merchant shrugs. "Weren't they? Didn't she have one about one of us wrestling a giant badger or something?"

"That was me," says the Ranger. "I did that. Last month."

The other three companions blink at her in genuine shock.

"Why?" asks the King.

"Don't ask."

None of them do. Instead, the Merchant continues with her arguments. "Fools often mistake vagueness for truth, which is why prophecy appears so promising. Why, I could devise my own mediocre poetry, if you'd like. What rhymes with 'gullible?'"

"I was working on that one the other day," the Barbarian sighs. "But I assure you, the Witch has—*had*—real magic. Not parlor tricks."

The Merchant glances about the space. "Isn't this a parlor?"

"Sitting room," says the King.

"Library," grunts the Ranger. She pulls a dried meat strip from beneath her cloak and holds it aloft. "Jerky?"

The others traveled with her long enough to know not to accept.

"The Ranger's interpretation sounds correct," the Barbarian admits. "One of us nine shall resurrect the Dark Lord, and since the Wizard, the Guide, the Captain, the Storyteller, and now the Witch herself are all dead, that leaves one of us four here. Now's our chance to save the future. Again."

"Put that on a poster," the King laughs. He stands and clasps his hands to his hips. "If we must play this game, then I'll start. I think it's the Merchant."

The Barbarian gasps. The Ranger frowns. The Merchant chuckles. The Witch continues being dead.

"Of course you'd accuse me," the Merchant says. "I'm the only person in this room richer than you. Must make you jealous."

The King paces back and forth like a lawyer before a jury. "I'll not dignify that claim with a reply."

"He replies," the Merchant quips.

The King glares at her. "My accusation is not without basis. You see, I received some intelligence recently, though I didn't know what to make of it until now. Tell us, Merchant. Why did you recently make a sizable acquisition of arms and armaments?"

The Merchant inspects her manicured nails. "Diversification is to business as milk is to bones. Also, your phrasing is redundant."

The Barbarian frowns. "Arms and armaments, though. Is this true, Merchant?"

"It is." The Merchant produces a quill from within her robes, then twirls it between her fingers with deft grace. "A speculative investment. Small immediate loss for potential future gain."

The King scoffs, tossing back his hair in a vaguely glamorous gesture. "What market is there in arms *or* armaments? Since we nine deposed the Dark Lord, mine is a land of peace. That was the whole point of the quest! Weapons are anachronistic. Surely you would only buy them if you had some insider information. If you were to, say, resurrect the Dark Lord and start a new war, perhaps? Or give birth to him."

"An amusing theory—especially the part about the evil baby. If you hadn't noticed, King, I'm far past my child-rearing days." She sighs. "I don't often open my books, but I'll do it for my oldest associates. Would you like to know the purpose behind my purchases?"

"Very much so," says the Barbarian. "Not that I'm accusing you."

The Merchant smooths her robes, making a faint clinking sound as she does. "Very well, then. It's for dinner theater."

"Dinner theater?" the King exclaims.

"Dinner theater?" the Barbarian repeats, his voice striking a squeaky note.

And then, just because he's so incredulous, the King says it again. "*Dinner theater?*"

"This room must be bigger than it looks, because it's got quite the echo. Yes, dinner theater. Specifically mock combat."

The King scoffs, but the Merchant carries on.

"We've no use for proper battles, true. But I've been conducting market research, and according to the results, public interest in combat remains. So why not a performance? Guests will dine and drink and enjoy choreographed duels while they do it. They'll sit in color-coded sections, each matching a combatant to root for. There should be souvenirs, too. I'm still working out the details."

"So we're supposed to take your word for this?" the King complains. "The word of a woman who'd tell a lie just for a copper?"

"A good lie is worth three coppers at least," the Merchant clarifies, "and if there's one thing you can trust me on, it's personal profit. I assure you, the Dark Lord was bad for my business. Subjugation, militarization, annihilation…why do you think I financed our expedition in the first place?" She leans forward. "Personally, I'm wondering if our King is a far more likely suspect."

"Me?" The King guffaws. "You embarrass yourself with such slander."

"Or perhaps she's onto something." The Barbarian touches a fist to his wrinkled chin. "I noticed your reaction when our dear departed Witch gave her prophecy. It almost looked like excitement in your eyes." He pauses, then adds, "Not that I'm accusing you."

"This is no way to speak to your liege."

"Then why do you seem so tense, your majesty?" the Merchant observes. She cocks her head to the side. "It's because you're sick of being King. Isn't it?"

"Nonsense," he laughs. But his laugh isn't as loud as it was before.

The Merchant studies the King like he's an abstract painting. "Forty years ago, when we were all liberating the world, you never once spoke of law, policy, diplomacy, or even trade routes. And trust me, I'd recall any talk of trade routes. You never wanted to be a king, did you? You just wanted the quest."

"Well," the King mumbles, "I suppose I enjoy a pounding pulse as much as the next man. But to accuse me of someday fathering a new Dark Lord just for the thrill of it? That's treasonous, Merchant. Not to mention tacky."

"I'm merely making an observation. You don't live for adventure—you need adventure to live. And it's been quite a while since this world offered any worthy ones."

The Ranger tightens the string on her longbow. "Is it you, King? Do you plan to father the Dark Lord?"

For a moment, the King is speechless. His tanned face goes from brown to red to purple. "You too, Ranger? You *all* think I'm guilty? Also, how does one *plan* to raise a Dark Lord baby, anyway?"

The Barbarian waves a hand. "I mean, I haven't technically accused anyone of anything…"

"I should have you all executed for this," the King murmurs. He stalks to the door.

The Ranger pulls her longbow taut once more. "Stop there."

The King turns, wide-eyed. "Folly. Treason. Attempted regicide!"

"I don't attempt. I hit what I aim for."

"Well, except that last shot," the Barbarian points out.

The Ranger growls at him in return. "We're too old to be saving the world again. Too spent to have its fate fall on us. But we've no choice. So no one leaves until we decipher the prophecy. Not even you, King."

"I'll have you all hanged for this," the King whispers, his face darkening like the shadows around them. "And then I'll have you quartered. Then incinerated. And then…something even more unpleasant. You cannot detain your liege. You won't."

"I'll do anything for my Realm. You know that. You all know that." The Ranger gazes at them with calm resolution. "If the Dark Lord rises again, we're all doomed. So if you're the one behind it, King, then I would gladly shoot you through the head. Any other questions?"

"I've got one." The Barbarian points at the books on the shelves surrounding them. "Why aren't we looking to stories to solve this riddle? They often contain answers to questions we're too afraid to ask."

But the King has already proceeded to a new suspect. "It's *you*, isn't it, Ranger?"

The Ranger looks about as concerned as ever, which is to say, not very. "What makes you say that?"

"Your manner. Your indifference to the prophecy. Your eagerness to accuse everyone else. You knew this was coming because you've been planning it all along. Now you're just framing a scapegoat. Or perhaps you've gathered us here to kill us." The King nods at the Witch's corpse. "Were you two working together? She sends the invitations, then you murder the guests? And double-cross her, too?"

The Ranger blinks slowly. "If it's me, then explain how I'll have a child at my age."

"Perhaps you won't. Perhaps you'll resurrect him."

"And how does one bring a dead man back to life?"

"Well, obviously, you'll, umm…" The King throws up his hands. "I don't know the mechanics of it! None of us do! We just know it'll happen—*if* we believe the Witch's prophecy, that is. Which I, for the record, do *not.*"

The Ranger peers down at her bow, running two fingers along the shaft. She plucks the string, making a surprisingly musical note. "I am a hermit. I live in the woods. Alone."

"Is that something to be proud of?" the Merchant asks.

"Yes. It's also my alibi. Even if I wanted to raise the Dark Lord, I don't have the means. But a King does. As does the richest woman in the world."

The Merchant laughs. "Money can buy death, true enough. Just ask any assassin. But no one can buy life, no matter how much they pay."

"Or can they?" The Ranger squeezes the shaft of her bow. "You could secure the services of a necromancer. Some of whom you've been known to employ, Merchant."

The Merchant shrugs. "There are lots of people on my payroll. Some might claim to be necromancers—I'd have to check their résumés. Perhaps you should ask our King; he and I have many contractors in common."

The King glares at her. "I shall not suffer this attack on my reputation. I am beloved, I'll have you know!"

"Because you happened to be the first king of a post-war age," says the Barbarian. "Just an observation, not an accusation. Also, general question. Why hasn't anyone accused *me?*"

The Ranger registers more surprise than she has all evening. "Do you want us to?"

"Well, it would be nice to be noticed, is all."

"Then consider yourself accused." The Merchant kicks her gilded boots up onto the table and stretches, hands behind her head. "Someone in this room is going to raise the Dark Lord. So what do we do about it?"

"'The first person shall triumph then,'" the Barbarian muses, squinting at the bookshelf as if the answer might be written inside. "The 'first person.' What do we think she meant by that?"

"It might refer to the first person who joined the quest," says the King. "Which would be you, Ranger. Wouldn't it?"

"I was the first to join, true. But the Wizard recruited me. So wouldn't that make *him* the first person?"

"Maybe," muses the Barbarian. "Anyway, the Wizard is dead. Very dead. We all saw what the Dark Lord did to him."

"Then what if it means the first person up the stairs of the Dark Lord's tower?" suggests the Merchant. "That was our great King, if memory serves."

"Well, it was really the Storyteller who went up first. We sort of walked in together, you know. Shoulder-to-shoulder. Besides, it was the Storyteller's idea for me to go first. Said it would make for a better tale. Besides, he's dead now, too."

"Is he?" The Merchant shakes her head. "Shame."

"Or what if it means the first person among us to be born?" asks the Barbarian. "The eldest of us."

"Wizard again," yawns the Merchant.

"Wasn't the Guide even older?" asks the Barbarian.

"No, it was the Captain!" says the King. "And besides, they're all dead now. Unless they can resurrect themselves, they're not giving birth to any Dark Lords. And that's only if you believe this prophecy, which I, for one—"

"Enough!" The Ranger slaps the table. "If we can't determine who the traitor is, there's only one solution left."

"Exchange firm handshakes and go our separate ways?" the King asks.

"No," answers the Ranger. "We must all forfeit our lives."

The Conclusion of the Conversation

"Excuse you?" says the King.

"Did she just say what I think she said?" says the Barbarian.

Even the Merchant, usually the very image of nonchalance, sits erect. "If this is a joke, Ranger, it's a poor one. Even for you."

"I've never told a joke in my life." The Ranger tosses her longbow on the table as if it's an offering. "We all know why we nine defied the Dark Lord. We meant to make this world a better place."

"And we did," says the King. "Look around! Looks a lot better than smoke and desolation, doesn't it?" He waves at the Witch's corpse. "Except for that. We'll get someone in here to clean her up."

"The Dark Lord's return will end our peace," the Ranger insists. "So if we can't determine who'll resurrect him, we must stand by the morals we claim to have. We must sacrifice ourselves for the good of the Realm."

"I'd rather not," says the Barbarian. "I haven't written my opus yet. Haven't even gotten to my late-life weirdo experimental phase."

"I won't do it, either," the King announces, turning up his chin. "The Realm needs its ruler."

But the Merchant only stares at the Ranger. "You truly mean this, don't you?"

In answer, the Ranger reaches into her bag and produces a vial. Inside swirls a writhing, murky substance, the same color as the night itself.

"That looks like poison. Is that poison?" The Barbarian stands and stumbles backward. "I don't like where this is going."

"Nor do I." The King flicks his hand. "Take it away. I command you."

Instead, the Ranger sets the vial on the table. "It's called 'Sweet Dream.' Painless. Quick. Like passing in one's sleep. It's the best way to go. All of us, together, like when we destroyed him the first time."

The Barbarian looks near the point of tears. "We can't sacrifice ourselves to kill a man who's already dead. The King's right. Our Witch must've been mistaken, or *we're* mistaken. Someone must be reading the signs wrong, or…or…"

But the Ranger does not argue with him. She simply takes a glass from each of the four settings at the table and pours poison into each.

"When I was young, my mother warned me life would pass faster than I knew. Her own sort of prophecy, and I ignored it. Now look at me. I'm old. We all are. We could sit here and wonder why we weren't better prepared, only we already know the answer. It's a great and simple irony, that the old have better foresight than the young, yet they've got less time to use it." The Ranger sighs. "Old as I am, I wouldn't mind getting a little older. But we've got a duty to leave this world better than we found it. And we're running out of time."

"Wow," the Barbarian gasps. "Nice monologue."

The Merchant studies the Ranger. "This would all be more compelling if you didn't poison the Witch."

"Poison?" the Barbarian gasps.

"The Witch?" the King adds.

Yet the Ranger reacts without so much as a pause. "She must've known she was dying. I had nothing to do with it."

"So you say. But even if one of us raises the Dark Lord, or gives birth to them, or becomes a new Dark Lord ourselves, wouldn't the Realm be stronger with its remaining heroes to defend it, old as we may be?"

"Collective self-sacrifice is the only way to ensure this fate never comes." The Ranger pushes the cups forward. "Drink. We must do it together."

"No. This reunion is over." The King strides to the door.

"You know I can't let you leave," murmurs the Ranger. "It could be you, even if you don't know it yet."

"And how will you stop me, hmm? By missing your shot again? You don't have the skill anymore, let alone the gall." The King opens the door.

"Forgive me," whispers the Ranger. And then she shoots the King. Not through the hand, and not through the door. This shot punches him through the right side of his head, just above his ear, where his crown might usually rest. The arrow stands there, quivering.

"Oh," he says. Blood trickles from the wound like a tear. "I think I've got something caught in my hair." He falls face-first into the door, slamming it closed, then he slumps there, like a drunk passed out for the night.

"What have you done?" the Merchant gasps.

"What needed to be done." When the Ranger turns to face the remaining two, there are tears in her eyes. "I didn't want this. Never wanted this. But her prophecies always come true. And if you won't drink…"

"It's just like the tragedies," moans the Barbarian. "Everyone dies at the end."

The Ranger pulls another arrow, pointing this time at the Merchant.

The Merchant dons that easy smile, which is admirable considering what just happened, and what's about to happen. "Let's talk about this."

The string twangs. The arrow strikes the Merchant in the chest, the shot generating such force that it knocks her off her chair and onto the floor. She lies there, facedown and motionless.

The Ranger loads another arrow, pulls the string…but the Barbarian is gone. Where? The room is small and the King's body still blocks the door. He must be hidden behind, or beneath…

The Barbarian springs up from under the table. The Ranger's arrow takes him in the shoulder, but it cannot stop his weapon, a tarnished old blade flashing from his belt and sliding between the Ranger's ribs with a sound like a whisper.

No last words for her. No smile on the way out. The Ranger topples backward and slumps into her seat, glassy eyes peering down at the weapon that killed her.

The Barbarian stands. He groans, clutching the arrow stuck in his shoulder. It's true, what the Merchant said: They're old now. Forty years ago, that shot would've taken him through the heart, killing him instantly. Instead, she missed. It's a painful wound, but not a mortal one, so long as he doesn't bleed out.

He doesn't plan to. He has a semi-autobiographical play to write about this experience.

With a howl, the Barbarian snaps off the shaft and bunches up his cloak, pressing it to his injury. He has to go, has to get back to his horse, to his own lands, where someone will tend to his wounds.

But first, the Barbarian lurches over to the Witch. "Was this all part of your plan? Is he back already, and you were his pawn, turning us against ourselves? Or do you really think I'll raise him back to power? Because it would have to be me, wouldn't it? I'm the only one left."

"Make that two," croaks a voice.

The Barbarian's head whips around, expecting another arrow to come sailing at his face, but it's none other than the Merchant, sitting up and looking winded, but very much alive.

"What evil art is this?" whispers the Barbarian. "Don't tell me you're a necromancer."

"No. I'm just prepared." She tears the arrow-hole in her robes wider to reveal twisted chainmail beneath. "Not the first time I've been shot at. Nor the last, I'd wager."

"So *that's* why you jingle. I always thought it was coins." The Barbarian offers a hand to help her up, then hesitates. "It's not you, is it?"

"If it was me, I would've killed you while you were soliloquizing just now. It's not *you*, is it?"

"You heard that?" He rubs the back of his neck, his cheeks reddening. "No, it's not me, either. If it was, I'd kill you now while you're recovering your breath."

He doesn't. Instead, he offers his hand, and she takes it. Together, they lurch to the door and haul the King's corpse aside. They stumble down the halls of the manor, clutching each other's shoulders as they go. They make it all the way to the front door, where they encounter the Witch's servant cleaning some entryway statues with a feather duster.

"How goes the reunion?" asks the servant with a pleasant smile.

"Messy," answers the Merchant. And she and the Barbarian lurch outside without another word.

<u>The Epilogue</u>

No one likes a prologue, but epilogues sometimes work, so long as there's something interesting left to say. And in this story, there is.

The Witch's prophecy is accurate, you see, as was the interpretation of our dead heroes. One of the nine shall resurrect the Dark Lord. But it isn't the Merchant, and it isn't the Barbarian. In fact, they'll be the only members of the original crew left in opposition.

But if not them, then whom? The two survivors contemplate this question as they ride.

"'The first person,'" the Barbarian quotes aloud. "That couldn't mean our firstborn child, could it?"

"If you're trying to woo me, you're doing a poor job." After a moment's consideration, the Merchant poses a theory of her own. "You're a writer, Barbarian. What if you were right about the books? After all, what does 'first person' remind you of?"

"The narrative voice, I suppose. I, me, my. The teller of the tale. But what tale might that mean?"

"I don't know," the Merchant admits.

I do. It's this one, of course. The one you're reading now.

So who am I, you ask? Who's telling this tale? Why, I'm the Storyteller, of course. I told the greatest story this Realm has ever known: the story of the nine who deposed the Dark Lord. Did I merely tell the tale as it happened? Or did my telling alter its outcome?

Any narrator has the power to manufacture truth, so long as the audience can suspend their disbelief. It's its own form of magic. If you, reader, are convinced by my story, then you must believe as my four friends did: that the Dark Lord shall rise again. I should know. I'm the one who's going to do it.

It won't be difficult. I'll resurrect him the same way I resurrected myself: by telling the tale.

See? Magic.

My dead friends would thank me, if they lived. I know the Merchant will, and the Barbarian. Heroes can't be heroes without villains. A world at peace is only a first act.

So now you know my secret. I could apologize for the surprise, but I won't. Life is full of surprises, after all, surprises that delight and frustrate. Are you delighted, reader? Are you frustrated? Will you stand in opposition, or will you join me?

Either way, none of us are getting any younger. And by now, someone should've warned you. Never trust an unreliable narrator.

Time after time, people are just who they seem to be. But occasionally, there's someone with the sort of layers that take you by surprise.

Take the actress Hedy Lamarr, for example. In the 1930s, she rose to stardom in Hollywood and was billed as the world's most beautiful woman. She starred opposite big names, like Clark Gable and Spencer Tracey, and eventually earned top billing over her male costars. Between filming, Lamarr designed and drafted inventions. Lamarr eventually patented a "frequency hopping" technology that served as the foundation for the wi-fi, Bluetooth, and GPS that we use today.

Another example is Samuel F. B. Morse, who invented a single-wire telegraph system and is famous for co-developing the code that bears his name. Morse code remains the standard for that type of communication to this day. Prior to being an inventor, however, Morse studied art at the Royal Academy in London, and was an accomplished painter, renowned for his portraits of people such as President James Monroe, and the Marquis de Lafayette, the leading French supporter of the American Revolution. Morse was appointed professor of painting and sculpture at the University of the City of New York in 1832, the first appointment of that kind in the United States.

Actor Jackie Chan is another layered individual, famous for his acting and comedic stunts in slapstick martial arts films. Chan attended the Peking Opera School, where he studied not only martial arts and acting, but also had vocal training. Chan has produced over twenty albums and has over one hundred songs that he has performed in five languages.

Who do you know who has layers?

BLOOD ROAD

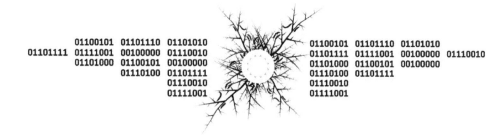

01100101 01101110 01101010
01101111 01111001 00100000 01110010
01101000 01100101 00100000
01110100 01101111
01110010
01111001

01100101 01101110 01101010
01101111 01111001 00100000 01110010
01101000 01100101 00100000
01110100 01101111
01110010
01111001

BY JESSICA RITCHEY

The chatter in the lobby wound through my head like the incessant buzz of flies on rotting fruit. I cursed myself again for forgetting my earbuds at home. The white noise machine at the receptionist's desk and the burble of coffee percolating did nothing to drown it out, and I had just reached my limit when—

"Ms. Cooper."

I rose and followed the stocky man in the navy suit to his office. I did my best to covertly breathe through my mouth, rather than endure the stench of ranch dressing and onions that filled the cramped space. I took the seat he gestured to and waited for him to speak. My heel bounced against the leg of the chair and the collar of my burgundy blouse chafed too close to my throat. I did my best not to tug on it. Did my best to listen as Mr. Dawson introduced himself. To look attentive as he laid a stack of papers before me and pointed to various paragraphs and clauses in the document.

The will.

Sharon's last will and testament.

When Mr. Dawson finished his monologue, he passed me a fountain pen. The loops that didn't resemble *Lucy Cooper* in the slightest flowed in smooth black ink from my practiced hand onto the page, and I scribbled the date beside it. Mr. Dawson signed his part, and then handed me a key ring with three keys of various sizes.

Back in my car, I closed my eyes and tugged on my shirt's collar as the afternoon sun soaked through the windshield. It was hard to accept that I was my cousin's sole beneficiary, but there were so few members of our family left that I wasn't really surprised. Sharon's vibrant spirit was stolen by sudden cardiac arrest at only forty years old, leaving all of her earthly possessions to me.

I sighed, pried my eyes open, and looked at the keys still clenched between my fingers. It would take me less than an hour to get there. I shot off a quick text to let John know I was done at the attorney and ask him to cover dinner for himself and the kids. *Will do. We love you,* he replied.

"All right, Coop, let's go."

I sped through the countryside with the music loud enough to drown out all thoughts, and one solo car jam session later, I pulled onto the packed dirt road for 533 Blood Road. Every small bumpkin town seemed to have some road or house with a gruesome moniker and no real notion of the name's origin.

I'd once asked Sharon if she'd ever gotten the story out of her parents regarding this particular road's name, and got a shrug and eyeroll in answer, along with, "Who knows what Pineville's founders were thinking." I hadn't bothered to press for details she clearly didn't know or care to find out.

It was the kind of road where residents walked along the chicory-fringed berm and waved to every passerby as if they'd known them a lifetime. I waved back, giving my best attempt at a genuine smile and not the tight-lipped half-assed grin I usually mustered. A quarter mile down the clay track, the cabin sat tucked back amongst the mountain laurel, columbine, and ground pine.

It lacked the warmth of lights in the windows now, of Sharon standing on the tiny front porch waiting to greet me with her messy bun and wide smile. I sat in the car for too long fighting the little voice in the back of my head telling me to just go home for now.

I brushed the thought away. As I stepped from my car, I was greeted by the sweet perfume of early-blooming crown vetch skating above the earthy aroma of decaying leaves. Birds trilled high in the trees, whose foliage dappled the ground in dancing spots of sunshine. The woods exuded *green*, the clean freshness of a summer day steeped in unburdened life, and I forced myself to take a breath and appreciate it.

As I climbed up to the covered porch, the boards of the front steps groaned beneath my weight. A breeze stirred the windchimes, whose vibrational tones sank into my skin, raising the hair on my arms.

I pulled the keyring from my pocket and fitted it to the lock on the front door. The bolt *snicked* as I turned the key, and the door creaked open. The air inside felt stale, but the scent of lavender and pine still traveled along the dusty motes that stirred upon my entrance.

I wanted to collapse onto the overstuffed couch, cover up with the thick crocheted blanket, and to put off sorting through everything for another day, another month. An imaginary day when I might have the luxury of relaxing as I meandered through Sharon's life. Instead, I opened all the windows and fixed the coffee pot to brew.

Two hours and three cups of coffee later, I sat in the middle of the living room area rug, surrounded by photos and cards, albums and mementos, letters and newspaper clippings softened with age. I scratched a yellowed strawberry sticker that had stiffly fallen off of an old handwritten essay on *Charlotte's Web*. The 'Berry Good!' aroma had faded into nothing but chemicals and dust, yet the nostalgia of simply seeing the sticker brought it back perfectly.

Amongst all the typical memorabilia, something struck me as odd. Sharon's diary—which she had started our sophomore year of high school and discarded within a year—had new entries beginning only a couple of months ago and continued through the day before her unexpected death.

I set the diary on the end table beside the sofa, then restacked all the other faded memories and packed them neatly back into the box from which they'd been exhumed. Darkness had fallen outside the cozy cabin, so I decided to call it a day. Over the weekend I'd be able to better catalog everything and decide what to donate, keep, or sell.

A breeze lifted my hair as I stepped onto the porch and pulled the door shut. Something rustled the underbrush, startling me. *Just a chipmunk.* I kept my eyes peeled, though, keys between my fingers as I descended the front steps. A chill ran through me, and I shivered. As my weight landed on the bottommost step, the board cracked. My instinctive scream faded to a hiss between my front teeth as the broken wood scraped the inside of my ankle, drawing blood.

"*Damnit.*" I took a steadying breath as I clenched the fabric over my heart and bent to examine the cut and the splintered wood that caused it. I made a mental note to pick up a board from Home Depot and bring some tools next time, as I hurried to my car.

Rocks pressed deep in the clay and fallen twigs popped and snapped beneath my car's tires on my drive back down Blood Road. It had been an exhausting day and, as I gave my half-assed smiles and waves to the same ambulatory neighbors, I vowed to do nothing but climb into bed as soon as I got home.

Three days later—Saturday—I returned to the cabin with tools and an ambition to make some real headway. Sharon had been a creative soul, and one who often frequented antique stores and flea markets in search of decorative trinkets. Needless to say, I had my work cut out. John had offered to come along and help, but I needed to do this on my own.

I contemplated starting on the broken front step first but decided against it.

Instead, I loaded my arms with bags, boxes, and packing tape, skipped over the broken board, and let myself into the house. Everything was just as I had left it. I put on a rock playlist and got to work cleaning and sorting.

The boxes, however, were slow to fill.

I found myself running my thumb over the jagged edges of rough crystal points, pulling the smooth knit yarn of an alpaca fleece scarf between my fingers, watching the sunlight filter through prisms and toss rainbows skittering across the walls, opening the cupboard doors over again just to hear the squeak of the hinges and mourn the fact that Sharon would never experience these things that she loved ever again. Tears pricked at the back of my eyes, and I swallowed hard against the lump in my throat. How could I possibly part with them?

The cottage didn't feel empty, not with all the pieces of Sharon's life still present. Bundles of dried herbs hung along the top of the kitchen window, their scents fresh and sweet and touched with the sharp tang of spice. They twirled slightly on an air current I couldn't feel, spinning on their tied axes a half-turn clockwise and then counter.

I lifted my finger, touching the inverted leaves and stilling them as I looked through the trees beyond the window and took a long stuttering breath. I released the air from my lungs, slowly willing the stab in my heart to leave with it.

Not for the first time, I contemplated what it might be like to live here, to step away from the noise of the city and keep all of this. The drive to work and to stores would be a hassle, but I would love to see my children grow up surrounded by this simple beauty. The quiet of the woods held an alluring weight. The kind of weight that could hold you still and offer bearing to your soul. I lowered my hand, and the bundle of nettle began its endless twisting once more.

After loading a couple boxes into the trunk of my car, I retrieved my toolbox and the board to fix the step. I measured and cut the new plank to length, then used the claw on my hammer to pry up the splintered wood. As I lifted the old board, I caught a glimpse of something metallic glinting from the earth beneath the porch. My heartrate spiked at the thought of reaching into that dark void. The harsh beam of light from my phone illuminated the space where I could make out a half-buried lockbox.

The black box was scuffed and dented in places, the paint had peeled from the corners and seams letting patches of rust bloom across the metal. The dirt around it didn't look packed down and settled as I would have expected if it had been there a long time, but maybe that was just because it wasn't exposed to the weather much.

Frowning at the discovery, I gripped the box's handle and tugged. The ground held tight and seemed to *tug* back. I released the handle quickly and sat back on my heels, wiping my hand on my jeans. The uppermost boughs of the trees around the cabin shivered as a gust of wind caught and tangled them. I squinted at the sky, the dark clouds gathering to the west.

"Hurry up, Coop." I tucked a loose strand of hair behind my ear and turned to the box again. I used the claw of my hammer to dig some of the soil loose around the edges and pulled it free. The metal clanged against the frame of the step, vibrating slightly as I turned it over and observed the lock.

"Hello," said a small voice.

I gasped and whirled, the box nearly slipping from my fingers. A girl stood on the flagstone path between the porch and driveway. Her hands were clasped neatly behind her back, and she rotated a little side to side, the skirt of her white dress twirling with the movement.

"Oh, you scared me!"

Her cheeks dimpled as she loosed a small giggle and twirled the chain of her necklace around a delicate finger. "I didn't mean to."

I looked beyond her, searching for a chaperone but found only the clusters of lacy ferns lining the drive. Around us, the forest quieted, listening, and my voice fell hushed to match. "Do you live nearby?" The closest house was about a quarter mile down the road.

"I'm just exploring." She stilled and her rich brown eyes rested on the box in my hands.

"Do your parents know you're out alone talking to strangers?" I tucked the box under my arm and her eyes tracked the movement. When she didn't immediately answer, I added, "You should probably head home so they know where you are."

"A storm's coming." She lifted her eyes from the lockbox to meet mine, then without blinking shifted her gaze to the sky.

"Right." I drew the word out, suddenly hyperaware of every sensation, every breath I took, the way the hinges of the box dug into the soft inner skin of my arm. I was also acutely aware of the distance between myself, this strange child, and the door at my back.

"Better get somewhere safe."

"So should you," I pointed out, although I had a feeling the girl, tiny though she was, could look after herself.

"Don't worry about me." Her cheeks dimpled once more, and then she turned and skipped down the drive back—presumably—the way she'd come.

I took the lockbox inside, then finished repairing the step and put the tools back in my car just in time for fat heavy raindrops to begin pelting the earth. I hurried into the dry cozy cabin, locked the door firmly behind me.

After swapping my t-shirt for a chunky oversized sweater, I poured a fresh mug of coffee, heavy on the cream and sugar. I plucked the lockbox from where I'd left it on the kitchen table and took a seat on the sofa, tucking my feet up beside me and watching through the living room window as the storm rolled in. I let the steam from my mug curl around my face before each sip, glad for the warmth as I listened to the wind whistle around the corners of the cottage.

The keyhole on the box was small—hardly bigger than a flimsy diary lock—but it held tight when I tried to pry it open. *I wonder.* Mr. Dawson had given me three keys. One to the cabin. One to Sharon's red and white 1978 Ford F-150.

And one I'd yet to find the lock it would open.

"Only one way to find out." I hopped up and took the keyring from the hook by the front door. The analog clock in the kitchen *tick, tick, ticked* away the seconds that I stared at the box, keys in hand, hesitating. "It's just a box." Saying it aloud would certainly make it true, no matter that the box had been shoved beneath the porch and haphazardly buried. No matter the odd girl who'd appeared when I'd found it. I glanced back to the door, triple checking the bolt was locked and the chain was across.

"Just try it."

I jabbed the key toward the lock, and it fitted perfectly. I assumed I would have to fight with the rusty box, to find just the right angle and force the lock open, but with the barest nudge of my fingers the key turned smoothly to the right with a satisfying *click.*

I blinked at my luck as my pulse drummed out a heavy rhythm, matching the *pat-pat-pat-pat-pat* of rain on the roof. I could feel it beating through the pads of my thumbs against the cool metal lid. Slowly, I lifted the lid, and the hinges screamed at me in protest, making my back teeth ache with the sound. The tang of metal filled my nostrils, the phantom taste of it coating the back of my throat as I inhaled.

"Oh," I breathed.

The inside of the box was lined with cushioned black velvet. And nestled into the thick cloth lay a dark metal spade, about six inches in length and attached to a slender decorative handle. Although it was about the size and shape of a garden trowel, the blade was too narrow and flat to be of much use tending plants. Plus, the metal appeared old, *very* old, and tarnished into an almost black patina.

My first instinct was to pick it up and inspect it, but instead I curled my fingers so that my nails pressed into the palm of my hand. Rain began pelting the window, smudging the woods outside into something reminiscent of an impressionistic painting. I thought there was a flash of white outside, but I blinked and it was gone. The hair at the nape of my neck stood on end, and suddenly I didn't want to sit alone in a cabin in the middle of nowhere in the midst of a storm. But it was late and I'd planned to stay.

I closed the lid of the lockbox and dumped it on the counter, wanting it out of my hands as quickly as possible. Then, I pulled all the curtains closed, afraid my imagination would run rampant if I watched the dark outside for too long. Instead, my eyes were drawn to the box on the counter. I scrubbed a hand down my face, if only for the excuse of forcing my eyes shut and away from the discovery.

I couldn't relax. Couldn't sit still. The cabin felt too small, too confining. I contemplated calling John, but he'd be getting the kids ready for bed, and I would only be one more chore to deal with.

So, I paced.

From the kitchen to the living room. To the bedroom. The bathroom. Bedroom. Again and again. The texture of the walls numbed my fingertips as I dragged them across the cool vertical planes. One hand and then the other, alternating between the walls and my teeth. My nailbeds were chewed near to bleeding by the time I paused.

The rain, and the unexpected dread that accompanied it, eventually lessened just past 11pm. I finally felt like I could breathe again.

Sharon's diary winked at me from where I'd laid on the end table and promptly forgotten about it in the midst of dealing with everything else.

I sat heavily on the sofa, turned on the little vintage TV/DVD combo, and scanned through the stack of video cases beside it. I settled on a movie I'd already seen four times. Something familiar and comforting. But the actors on the screen couldn't hold my attention, and my mind drifted back to the evening's events. The box. The girl. The storm. The blade.

The dagger—for that's what I had convinced myself it was—had seemed to emanate malice and made my skin itch. I didn't even want to look at it again just yet. Instead, I pulled Sharon's diary toward me across the stand. Neon peace signs and big stylized daisies decorated the cover of the journal. The lock was long gone, so I undid the metal clasp and flipped the book open. Sharon's handwriting in high school had been precise bubbly cursive.

> *Jan. 1ˢᵗ, 2000*
>
> *Happy New Year! We all thought the world was going to end last night. It didn't. Y2K was a load of propagandic bullshit. If you ask me, what we should really worry about is why two teens decided to take their school by firestorm…*

Typical Sharon. Couldn't have given a rat's ass less about whether technology would continue but give her a real tangible humanitarian problem to worry over and she'd obsess. I thumbed through some pages.

> *April 15ᵗʰ, 2000*
>
> *Tax Day! Just ask the rents. Really wish they would chill, it's*

like they totally forget this day is coming every year. We're going to the cabin for the weekend so Dad can clear his mind and forget about "financial responsibilities." Really, I think he just wants the excuse to go trout fishing and drink beer...

April 17th, 2000

Today was weird. Like, really weird. Dad was only fishing for a couple of hours when he came back. He wouldn't talk to Mom and his hands were covered in mud. And I swear—honest to God—I swear there was blood on his shirt. I can't stop seeing it. The blue and white flannel with splotches of red.

Mom's crying in the kitchen right now because Dad's shut himself in the bedroom. She keeps saying, "Can't be. It can't be," and she won't tell me what she's talking about.

April 18th, 2000

Dad seemed almost normal today. He sent mom and I home and said he needed some time alone, but he wouldn't look at me until I tried to make a joke about the irony of being bloody on Blood Road. His face went pale and he told me to never say that again. Why do old people have to be so uptight all the time? Couldn't he see how freaked out I really was? A little humor never hurt anyone.

That was the last entry from 2000. A few pages following it had been ripped out. Then, a more elongated hand, the letters stretched thinner by years and experience.

April 1st, 2024

I can't believe Mom kept this diary all these years. She's gone now. Passed away two years ago from cancer. I remember the night she took this little book. I'd been asking questions about where Dad was and what was wrong with him—the reclusiveness and irritation had only gotten worse after that weekend at the cabin. She'd snooped through my room, found my diary, and I never saw it again.

I was doing some spring cleaning today, and found it

wrapped in an old tea towel and stashed at the bottom of a box of old photo albums.

April 5th, 2024

I'd forgotten how enjoyable journaling can be. Just me, my thoughts, and this little book…

April 9th, 2024

I found something. Dad had said not to dig. He'd said it over and over.

April 10th, 2024

Dad was right.

Some things are much better left buried.

That was it. I snapped the diary shut.

Buried. Like the box had been? Why hadn't she ever told me that story about her dad and the fishing trip? I was sure I'd remember if she had.

After a night spent tossing and turning, I brewed *another* full pot of coffee, filled a giant mug with steaming liquid energy, and stepped out the front door in search of answers.

As I got my toolbox from the backseat of my car and waved to yet another person walking along Blood Road past the end of the driveway, I caught sight of my reflection in the car window and cringed at the grimace I'd thought had been a friendly smile. *No more smiles.* My cheeks heated at how foolish I must look to all of Sharon's neighbors.

The storm had blown branches through the front yard and scattered them across the cabin roof. The ground and sidewalk were still wet and puddled from the rain, but I wasn't going to let a bit of water deter me. I couldn't shake Sharon's mention of digging. I'd thought at first it was metaphorical, that she'd been asking too many questions. But what if the meaning was literal? It needled at me.

I set to work undoing my repairs from the day before, determined to find out if anything else had been in the ground alongside the lockbox. I shined my flashlight farther under the porch, where the dirt lay in dry gray clumps untouched by the rain, but there wasn't much to see. So, I began scraping around the hole I'd pulled the box from with a small garden trowel.

"Well, hi there, ma'am," a low and slow drawl came from right behind me.

I squawked in alarm and spun around.

"Need a hand with anything?" He was older than me, maybe close to 50, wearing a stained blue ballcap, overalls, and black rubber waders.

"Good lord." I pressed a hand to my forehead. "Folks around here sure do know how to startle a girl."

"My apologies, Miss …?"

"Lucy," I supplied. "Lucy Cooper." I dusted my hands on the fronts of my jeans and held my hand out to shake.

The man shoved his hands into the front pockets of his overalls and smiled, showing all of his tobacco-stained teeth. "A pleasure, Miss Cooper. Name's Dan."

I dropped my unmet hand back to my side. "Nice to meet you, Dan. Haven't had a chance to introduce myself to many of the neighbors, but I've seen you walking. Did you know Sharon?"

"We were acquainted. Such a shame. Odd girl, though, that one."

"She had some quirks—"

"You family of hers?" he interrupted.

"Yeah, she was my cousin."

He nodded, the nostrils of his large nose flaring. He pulled a hand from his pocket and looked at his watch. "Welp. I best get going. Time's a tickin'."

"Thanks for stopping by, Dan."

"I'm sure I'll see you again soon." He strolled around my car and down the drive.

I shook my head. *And he said* Sharon *was an odd one.*

I returned to my digging, moving earth from the sides and bottom of the hole. I found a few worms, a couple of beetles, and one horrifically large wolf spider, but nothing manmade.

However, I wasn't about to give up that easily.

I widened my dig site until all the dirt beneath the steps had been overturned, and my fingers tangled around a delicate silver chain. Carefully, so as not to break the tiny links, I pulled it from the soil. From the chain dangled a heart-shaped silver locket. My blood flushed cold through my veins, despite the sun scorching the back of my neck.

I set the locket on top of my toolbox and decided I needed to keep going. It could all be fixed, put back together like a puzzle, after all.

One by one, I pried up the floorboards of the porch and stacked them to the side. I didn't let myself think of the mess I was making, the mess I would have to clean up, or what I might do if I uncovered something truly grisly.

I found a full-sized shovel in the shed beside the cabin and just kept digging. Spearing the shovel into the dirt. Stomp. Scoop. Repeat. Blisters formed on the palms of my hands, breaking open and seeping against the wooden handle of the shovel, but the pain didn't stop me. Spear, stomp, scoop, repeat. Neat rows over and over, uncovering all manner of trinkets and baubles.

The necklace.

A tie pin in the shape of a fox's head.

A pewter compact.

Reading glasses.

A wristwatch.

A silver belt buckle inlaid with turquoise stones.

I wanted to believe that they were family heirlooms, that they'd fallen between the cracks of the floorboards over the generations by grandparents, aunts, and uncles. I wanted to believe it, but I couldn't.

It was near dusk by the time I'd finished, but the setting sun didn't cause the chill that ran through me. I snapped a picture of the items and sent it to John with the message, *There's something weird here.*

He replied, *Something weird like ripping apart a porch?? Should I come help?*

Are you okay?

"You found it." I jumped at the voice. It was the little girl again, and she was pointing to the locket.

"I found lots of things." I took a small step back and regretted it when she smiled.

"You've been *very* busy."

"What are you doing here?" I asked perhaps a tad more sharply than I should have. So, I added more gently, "It's almost dark."

"I'm talking to you, what's it look like I'm doing?" Her voice lost the girlishness and my skin prickled.

"Go home." If she wasn't playing anymore, neither was I.

She sighed and took a step closer. "Home is calling. Do you hear it?"

"Stop." My voice shook around the word, the authority I'd meant to convey sliding away.

Her cheeks dimpled. "I just want it back. Can you give it to me?"

"Give what to you?" The door into the cabin was a good three feet above ground level, and I regretted pulling up the floorboards, not only for the now difficult escape.

"Anything here I can help with?" A large form in overalls and waders lumbered up behind the girl.

"Oh, Dan! Do you know where this girl belongs? She really needs to get home. And so do I, actually."

"Catherine's just impatient. Don't you worry a bit, Miss Lucy."

"Impatient for what?"

"For you to get the call of course, silly." Catherine's cheeks dimpled, the tone of innocence back. Her eyes, however, told a different tale as they shifted to the boxes beneath one of the butterfly bushes surrounding the porch.

I sidestepped slightly, blocking her view.

"I told you home is calling."

"Yeah, I do need to get home. So, if you'll both excuse me." I didn't want to turn my back on them, but my car keys were on top of the toolbox. I bent to retrieve my belongings, and as my fingers brushed the lid of the box, something *pulsed* within.

"Give me my locket." Catherine suddenly stood over my crouched form, demanding.

"You're wearing your locket." I lifted both boxes into my arms, my keyring dangling from my pointer finger.

"My *real* locket." She snarled the words at me.

"Excuse me?" I shifted my keys, the cool metal of their blades nestling between my fingers as I closed my hand into a fist.

"I don't like repeating myself." She batted her long dark eyelashes at me.

I looked at Dan, hoping for some sense of reason, some help with whatever game this wicked child was playing.

"Well, you see Miss Lucy, we just want our things. And then we'll be on our way." He looked past me to the support beam where I'd laid out all the trinkets I'd found.

Behind Dan, another figure appeared. A woman in a calico sundress, her blonde curls pinned neatly to the side of her head. She nodded in agreement with what Dan said. A man appeared to my right, stepping from the shadows of the mountain laurel and tipping the brim of his hat. His faded blue jeans were held up by a belt with the gaudiest turquoise buckle.

I didn't dare look away to see if it was still on the beam behind me, but I swore I'd dug that very belt buckle from beneath the porch. *Impossible.* More figures appeared, and the lockbox pulsed again, as if the lid strained to open from the inside. I clutched it tightly to my chest to keep from dropping it.

"Take them," I gasped. "Just take whatever you want and leave me alone."

Was this how Sharon had died? I feared for my own heart's welfare as it hammered against the lockbox, and the lockbox seemed to hammer back. No. That wasn't the box, it was the dagger knocking to be released.

"We can't just take them." Dan looked at me sadly.

The box slipped from my arms and crashed onto the walkway, the lid springing open and the dagger tumbling out. I scrambled to grab it before any of the others in the yard could get it and use it against me. Once my fingers wrapped around the hilt, I couldn't let it go. Its pulse wormed its way through the palm of my hand, up my wrist and crept into the very fibers of my muscles. It snaked up my arm, demanding.

The blade had a thirst.

My arm, my hand, they were not my own. I willed my fingers to uncurl, to let the dagger fall, but they did nothing but hold tighter. There was a *pull*. As there had been when I first found the box. The blade *needed*.

"There's no one else." Catherine said softly, her dark eyes filled with delight. "You feel the call now, don't you?"

My mouth gaped open, horrified, before I managed to ask, "No one else?"

"No one else *alive*. Not for miles and miles." She giggled. "We're all right here…"

It was fully dark now, but I could see the clearing around the cabin was filled.

The dagger hummed with power and *need*. My mouth dried with sudden thirst.

"You can't deny it," a voice whispered.

"It finds a way."

"It always finds a way."

The cacophony of their voices surrounded me, burrowing its way through my eardrums, unendingly grating and goading me until I couldn't take it another second.

"*What do you want?*" I screamed, squeezing my eyes closed.

Silence met my ears. I opened my eyes to find the point of the dagger pressed against my throat. It wasn't cold, as I might have expected, but warm as if it had been bathed in hot blood. The tip of it pricked my skin, drawing tears to my eyes, as the now quiet audience watched on.

"It can't be me. Don't take me. *Please don't take me.*" My voice broke, ending in a sob.

The fingers of my left hand clawed at those of my right, trying to break their grip on the handle, to shove the blade away from the tender flesh of my throat. I backed away from my own hand until I met the frame of the porch and toppled backwards into my dig site. The newly overturned earth softened my fall, clods of dark soil pressed against the side of my face, making their way into my mouth and nose as I gasped for air and continued to press as far from the dagger as I could.

My fall had knocked over the souvenirs I'd excavated. Inches in front of my nose was a splash of turquoise against the dirt. I scrambled to grab the hideous belt buckle and my trembling fingers slipped against the smooth tarnished silver. Finally, I managed to get a firm grip and jammed the buckle as hard as I could between the tip of the blade and my throat. The dagger pierced the silver and would have continued through my trachea, but I gripped the buckle with all the strength I could muster and twisted it sharply back.

Snap.

My right hand sprang open, releasing the blade, which toppled harmlessly to the ground in two silent pieces. My breath sawed in and out of my lungs and I scrunched my eyes shut as the cool night air stung the cut on my throat.

As pale sunlight peaked between the trees against the eastern sky, I prodded the glowing orange logs in the firepit. Then, I quickly scanned the email draft to Harmon & Smith Real Estate once more before hitting send.

The cabin sat at my back and the woods around me were quiet. Free. Cleansed by the dew of a new day. Mixed within the pine and maple ashes, and beneath the flames lay the warped and melted remnants of the dagger and its souvenirs. The ghosts were gone. To where, I had no way of knowing.

But I knew none of us would set eyes on Blood Road ever again.

ERROR CODE 9-927: FRUSTRATION ALERT

Citing section 31B subsection 5R of the Puzzlers Code, a note on perseverance:

Dedication to a task can come with great reward. Not all problems have easy solutions, but those that initially prove difficult can be the most rewarding to solve. Frustration may occur, and indeed may tempt even the most resolute players into quitting. The Puzzler's Association would like to recognize that frustration is a common occurrence and would like to take this opportunity to formally remind all players that staying dedicated and using the tools at their disposal may help them move through the feeling of frustration.

An Accounting of the Marchioness

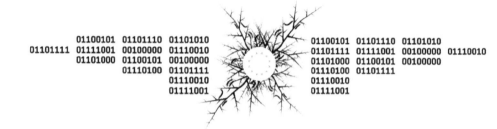

01100101 01101110 01101010
01101111 01111001 00100000 01110010
01101000 01100101 00100000
01110100 01101111
01110010
01111001

01100101 01101110 01101010
01101111 01111001 00100000 01110010
01101000 01100101 00100000
01110100 01101111
01110010
01111001

BY AMANDA PICA

I carried the candle in my left hand, always the left, and used my right to tighten my robe where it threatened to fall open at my collarbone. The back staircase of my family home wound in a tight and angular spiral into darkness. Grandmother would have been appalled to find me in nothing but nightclothes, slipping down stairs meant only for the feet of our staff. No doubt she would have understood my task, though by Mother's account, she'd been able to do such unsavory things in the light of day.

No fires burned at this time of night, and the drafts assumed their rightful September place. My bones sang with the cold, and I clutched my robe tighter.

Behind the kitchens, I heaved on a wrought iron ring until the heavy door opened enough to slip through. Another set of stairs. Darkness, astride me in parallel lines, followed me down to the cellar floor. My candle's light reached the cellar corners but not into the vaulted ceiling. I scanned the manor's winter stores: barrels of root vegetables, grains, and bottles of wine set or stacked in sets of five. I nodded once. Five was right, but nausea still rippled through me in waves of both repulsion and need.

My slipper-clad feet whispered across the stone floor, barely audible over the murmurs that swirled around me. Every tendon in my body stretched taut and warned me away. As I approached the westernmost corner, bile rose into my throat. Stone block comprised almost all of the manor house with deftly hewn straight lines through-out, except here, where it twisted this way and that. The slithering curves lead to five stones atop one another, oddly faded at their edges, as though I looked at them with eyes that swam with tears. Their serpentine lines belied their strength. The twists and turns, the very wrongness of this place, had gotten substantially worse over the last year. It required more and more from me, until at times I felt there may be nothing more to give.

I swallowed. The foul bile lingered in my mouth and burned the soft flesh at my throat. Only two days hence since my last trip down, and it had progressed this much. My dear Edward had watched over me all last night and had prevented me from coming here. His heart longs to help that which his mind cannot comprehend, and heaven help us, but it grows in strength with every passing day.

One step closer to the stones and my stomach lurched harder. I spun and vom-ited into the first vessel available, a wooden bucket, then wiped my mouth with the back of my right hand three times. One was not enough and both two and four were too weak. White dots swam in my vision.

My flickering flame lit the stones and their surface ate the candlelight. I crouched and put the candlestick on the ground to free my left hand. It was always my left. Unformed images of undulated masses swam and plunged through my conscious-ness. Flashes of scale, tooth, and claw. Far too many blood-tinged eyes.

I shook my head. The beasts were not here. Not now. Not ever, if I had any say at all.

I tapped the stones with three fingers in rapid succession for a total of thirteen sets.

One, two, three, four, five.

As I tapped, the visions faded and relief enveloped me. In it, the weight of my exhaustion pulled on my resolve. I picked up my candlestick and hurried back up and up and up to my bedchamber where I extinguished the light and slipped into bed next to Edward. The stones would quiet until tomorrow evening, by my calculation. A far shorter duration than last year at this time, but long enough that I'd finally rest.

On the arrival of morning, dear young Beatrice woke me while tending the fire in my bedchamber's hearth. I waved away her apologies, then asked her to bring a container of water. The bile from last night lingered still and I wished to rinse it away. She scuttled off.

The sun's angle that cut across the floor indicated mid-morning, and the linens next to me were cool. Edward must have been up for some time. He suspected my travels in the night, more so now than in any of the past year since we'd wed. I prayed his prior night's vigil would ease his worry enough to let me be, and that his deep slumber last night came from a place other than simple exhaustion.

I folded back my blanket and linens, rose and dressed in the solitude of the autumn morning. Clothing hung just so in my wardrobe; each left sleeve draped over the back of the garment. The tasks came to me as whole and complete things, as sure of themselves as the giant sycamores that stood on the forest edge. All I ever knew was that the world stayed solid when I performed them.

Beatrice returned with a small pitcher of water and two glasses. She made no eye contact with me, and I questioned her about it. I hadn't known her long, but she normally had a friendly countenance. She merely curtsied, an awkward motion on her spindly legs, and disappeared out the door.

I sat on the ornate chaise lounge nearest to the fire and stretched my legs out. A cat warming in the sun. The fire's crackle proved worthy company, certainly better than the inane pattering of the occasional cousin who dropped by with their false well-wishes. I knew they visited to size up my holdings and calculate their place in the family line. Perhaps one such had beguiled Beatrice in a letter and turned her against me. Those greedy fussocks hadn't the courage I did, nor the strength to assume this compulsory role. I would choose the peace of a village shack over the work I did at the manor as the guardian of this world, had I the luxury of choice. I shifted on the chaise and flipped my hair over my shoulder. I counted the logs in the fire and there were only four, so I added a fifth and sat back down and stretched my legs again, this time with some effort. This wilting body betrayed me.

"My darling?" Edward poked his head into the doorway and a lock of his dark hair fell askew down his forehead. "Might I bother you?"

"Dear Edward. You cannot ever be a bother. Come, sit."

I swung my legs down to the floor, a gesture of balance and good health if ever there was one, and made certain to keep the grimace off my face. I glanced at him to make sure he noticed.

"Violet!" Edward placed a tray on a nearby table and rushed forward, arms out as though to catch me from toppling into the fire.

"I am perfectly fine. Please, stop treating me like I sit at death's door."

"Dearest," Edward said as he always did at the beginning of a speech about my health, "I only worry so."

I cut him off with a tut-tut. He took my hand and entwined my fingers in his, and the contrast of my paleness against his tanned skin stood stark in the firelight. He smiled, and before I could protest about how very well I felt, I lost all my contrary words.

He loved me, and that was enough.

I leaned my head against him and drew my knees up on the chaise. I breathed him in, pine and leather and petrichor, and he stroked the length of my hair. So at peace in those moments of repose, I would have frozen time. The day had darkened behind cloud cover and gave my bedchamber the promise of twilight instead of midmorning, and the dim light lulled me with contentment.

Edward nudged me and when I sat up, he stood.

"My heart, I have something for you since you missed breakfast."

He brought the silver tray over from the table nearest the door, piled with cheeses, fruits, and bread. I took to it with gratitude. I stacked the foods three pieces high, so each mouthful had a bit of apple, a bit of cheese, and a bit of bread. Though

I suspect he tried to hide it, Edward reveled in my every bite, unaware that keeping me from the cellar stones also kept me from my appetite. He declined to join me, protesting that he'd broken his fast in the dining hall earlier. Once finished and quite full, I nestled back into my beloved's warm shoulder and again he stroked my hair. The peace of the moment closed like a perfectly proportioned box around me until we were interrupted by the clearing of a throat.

"Excuse me."

"Marwood? Yes?"

"M'lord, a moment of your time?"

Mr. Marwood, the head butler of the manor, waited in the shadows of the hallway. He'd learned to be near invisible under the weight of Father's storied expectations all those years ago and had never changed. I'd never known Father's strict ways for myself; an accident had taken him in the months prior to my birth. Edward and I preferred to keep a more modern house than what I understood Father to have done. Fewer staff, fewer formalities. Mr. Marwood had been known to grumble about this, though never to our faces, yet still I knew he blamed my lack of fatherly influence.

"Darling Violet, I'll return as quickly as possible." Edward squeezed my hand.

"No need. I've rested long enough. I rather feel like walking in the gardens today."

Edward leveled me with a look so serious that I laughed, and in response, a frown tugged his handsome face into lines and creases.

I patted his hand. "I know that you worry. Perhaps you could meet me outside and we could walk together."

Edward's nod shook loose the crinkle in his brow. "Come to my study before you go out. Whatever Mr. Marwood needs may be quick, and if so, I can join you. Pray the weather holds."

Alone again, I debated changing into something warmer. Many of my garments hung too loosely on me now, thanks in part to the wretched vomiting caused by the stones. I did not wish to garner more worrisome looks from Edward; instead, I hoped to ignore all those heavy thoughts this morning and pretend we were courting again. I could use a bit of joy. I layered a thick wool coat over my dress and tied the belt around the waist. The fabric hugged me and forgave my shrinking body.

Despite my high mood, I took no flippant chances. I stepped over the seams made by the blocks of stone pressed together on the floor. **I stepped with my left** foot **first onto and off every rug.** At the arched entryway leading to the grand hall balcony, I tapped the two leftmost stones that had our family's crest etched into them. I walked nearest to the railing of the balcony and counted the spindles. I blinked at every third one.

I followed the railing all the way down the main curved staircase, and at the bottom, I paused at a vase of fresh flowers that adorned a small table. I tilted my head to examine the bouquet. It nudged me so gently, the flutter of a wing, so I experimented with the blooms. This way and that, but nothing felt right. I pulled two stems of aster from the water in the vase, to leave seven instead of nine. I laid them on the table, stems touching, with one bloom to the right and one to the left. The nudging fell away and when contentment filled its place, I could move on.

At my husband's study, my hand on the knob, an unexpected voice seeped out between wood and stone. I retracted my hand and hovered, much like the manor ghost some accused me of being.

"Surely that extreme measure is not necessary," Edward responded to the other man. Anger shaped each word into a verbal weapon.

"My Lord, it is. Her wasting disease has gotten worse, and at a time when she ought to be gaining for the sake of the child."

I touched my belly. Could it be?

"My Lord, do not make me repeat myself about her mental state. Forgive my impertinence, but I am the doctor here."

Ah. The mystery voice belonged to Dr. Greggson. I narrowed my eyes. He had accused Mother of being cracked without a shred of consideration for her claims. She'd still be alive if he had just listened, and I'd have been able to complete her tutelage of the stones. Instead, I'd been left alone, motherless, to figure it out for myself.

Edward's voice, now a low growl, rolled like fog over the moors.

"She is the Marchioness and more so, she is my wife. I will not condone her being locked up like some common beast."

"As you wish, my Lord. Keep her here, observe her, and be prepared to reap what you've sown."

Footfalls moved toward the door, so I ducked down an unused servant's corridor past where shadow intersected light. The door flung open and Greggson's heavy footfalls disappeared toward the front of the house. More footfalls followed and once they'd passed, I peeked out of the corridor. Marwood. I counted to twenty-three, a very strong number, to slow my breathing.

When calm came, I stepped into the study. Would he tell me now, or wait until our stroll through the garden? Edward stood at the far window with a glass of brandy in one hand. A smile eased onto my face. How delighted he'd be to share this news, and I'd give him the gift of pretending I hadn't already overheard.

"Dear husband. Shall we walk?"

He did not turn around. "I'm not of the mood. The sky is ominous and we'd be best to stay inside."

My smile faltered. "Shall we perhaps…" I began, hoping to offer chess in the library or perhaps to read to him like I used to do, but the words did not immediately come. His shoulders had rounded. Four zinnias sat amidst chamomile in a curved vase on one of eight shelves in his study. My skin prickled. This was the one room of the manor I could not fix.

"I've work to get done, my darling. I'm sorry. Please close the door behind you." Edward set down his drink, and the sharp sound of glass on wood matched the clipped tone of his voice.

Dejected and confused, I closed the heavy door with a click, tapped thrice on the knob with my left forefinger, and went to the library alone. He not only kept the information from me, but he seemed so vexed over what should have been joyful news. I mulled this over and over, my mind a rat gnawing through a wall, while pacing the bookshelves and tapping the spine of every third tome, alternating between the top and the bottom.

"My Lady?"

I whirled around, and young Beatrice took a step backward with her eyes wide.

"Oh, dear, I'm sorry. I startled you. You startled me, you see, and I…" I shook my head. "Please. Come in."

I crossed the room, left foot on the rug first, and sat on the sofa that had three pillows, careful not to touch any of them. Beatrice came to my side.

"I'm to see if you're hungry, m'lady."

"Did Mr. Marwood send you?"

"Yes, m'lady."

I tapped my finger in sets of three on the arm of the sofa. One-two-three. One-two-three. Marwood had not only been in the room but had called Edward to the meeting in the first place.

"My husband brought me a lovely fare but an hour ago, perhaps two, so I can wait until tea to eat. Tell me Beatrice, what are the rumors of my health?"

Beatrice dropped her gaze. "Not mine to say, m'lady."

I gave her a long glance and her palpable discomfort gave me pity. "So be it. Should you have a change of heart, I would be ever so grateful."

Days stretched to weeks, and Edward pulled away further as time passed. He haunted his study and left me to take all my meals alone in the dining hall under the watchful eyes of former Marquesses frozen in oils on canvas. Not even one former Marchioness adorned the walls, despite the eldest women in our family line doing the hardest of the work. I longed for their support and wisdom but couldn't even take solace in their image.

I appeased the stones by night and gnawing uncertainty by day. My growing loneliness made the enormity of the hall unbearable, and after enduring it as long as I could, I took my meals in the library instead. The manor's chill, worsened by the absence of Edward's warmth, sent me in search of what coziness I could find.

"Beatrice," I asked on one particularly long afternoon. "What news of the outside?"

Beatrice furrowed her brow. "Why, I haven't any, m'lady. All letters are still delivered directly to m'lord's study, as he'd asked."

"Oh, oh yes. Of course. I'd forgotten."

Edward was denying everyone in the manor their correspondence. Best to pretend I already knew that bit of madness—no sense creating new rumors about the state of our marriage. Edward still had not told me Greggson's news about a baby, despite now being far enough along to feel the changes. What a fool he must think me to be, unaware of the timing of my own courses. He dared to keep this news of my body from me, along with all other news as well, it seemed. Irritation surged through me.

I placed both feet firmly on the floor and lifted my heels five times each, first left, then right. I loved Edward. There must remain my focus. Weakness of my resolve gave the stones power.

I kept my expression level as I looked back at Beatrice. "Has Dr. Greggson been about?"

Beatrice tilted her head, and the slight gesture offered a glimpse into her as a person beyond the stiff formality Marwood's tutelage caused.

"Are you unwell, m'lady?"

"No. Never mind. Please, though, make me aware of his next visit?"

"I will m'lady. Might I be excused? I've work downstairs."

"Of course."

With Beatrice gone, I had naught but the patter of endless rain outside to keep me company. No birds flew in these late autumn storms. The instability of my marriage swirled inside me, a spiral of curves that twirled out of control. I paced the shelves again, as I had every day before, counting and tapping. Each shelf contained an odd number of books but I mustn't be lax; anyone might borrow a book from the room when I'm not about. I've not missed a night at the stones in as many weeks as Edward's secret had kept us apart, and the visions should have been stayed, but they flit on the edges of my awareness at all times of day now. The blended times, the times perpendicular to midday and midnight, housed the worst of them.

Even the gardens were kept from me, further compliments of this dreadful weather. How long could storms linger over one house? I strode to the large window, hung with heavy draperies, and the staccato sound of the rain on the glass bore into my skull. I longed for the carriage of a blasted cousin to come round the way. Even someone who treated me like a fragile thing and peppered me with questions would be a welcome change to this forced isolation.

I put my hand to my belly as I had so many times lately. My only companion. Perhaps it was selfish to seek unconditional love from a child when my husband refused me. Guilt looped around me and I dropped my hand. I closed my eyes to let tears gather as they would behind my eyelids, but none came. Instead, I squeezed my hands into fists.

Edward did not get to choose this life for me. This was my family home, and he brought nothing to it save for warmth and love. Marrying for wealth and stature would have been the wiser choice. Marwood believed so, underneath his stoic countenance. Yet I married a soldier from a lesser family because he charmed me so with his kindness and care, which I hadn't felt in all these weeks. He did not get to take that from me.

I stormed from the library, bound for Edward's study, determined for answers. Slight movement fluttered in the shadows and I passed it off as nothing. I wasn't ready to let go of the powerful feeling my righteous anger gave me. The powerful distraction. As I closed the distance, a swell of whispers washed over me. Perhaps Edward had someone in his study again, an unlikely thing since I'd have seen a carriage from my post at the library window. I continued on my way, still careful to step in all the correct places despite my anger. I only paused to tap the family crest where it was carved to the left of one arched doorway. As I neared the study, the whispering grew more distant.

It couldn't be.

I backtracked, and my focus on the whispers dampened the fire my anger had lit. Their volume rose as I retraced my steps, and the noise led me down the main stair toward the kitchens. Toward the cellar door. I stopped with the realization and shivered when a wash of spring runoff flooded my veins. I'd never heard them anywhere but the cellar before. Tiny pinprick sensations rippled over my skin and scalp and grew with intensity until I could not tolerate them, the unbearable feeling of biting insects and twisting snakes. I thrashed and scratched at my head and ruined the braid Beatrice had twisted into my hair. I pushed up my sleeves and scratched up and down my arms. I dug hard at the itch, seeking relief that did not come. The nearer I grew to the cellar door, the stronger the whispers. I cocked my head, trying to make out words but the guttural, visceral sounds seemed to have too many vowels to make sense of. I felt the stones in the cellar as though they were threaded to my very core, tugging at me.

Tugging at my unborn child.

I grasped my abdomen and spun around, then lifted my heels in rapid succession. The power in the stones had been growing all this time, as I'd suspected, but they had been holding back. They'd lain in wait until I'd let my guard slip, my distraction about Edward, and now they challenged me when they perceived me to be weak. I tapped my belly with my left finger in sets of three while I rapidly whispered a sequence.

Three, five, seven, eleven.

Thirteen. Seventeen.

I fought to hold the lock tight and swayed from the effort. I squeezed my eyes closed. I could not succumb to a fainting spell now. I needed to shove the whispers back to give myself time to get to the stones and perform the most powerful and most draining of all my tasks by touching them directly.

"Violet?"

I opened my eyes. Edward and Morwood stood in the archway to the kitchens, both agape. I sped up again. I hadn't gotten through the numbers yet. Not finishing a set might be catastrophic and cause the sort of crack in the mortar that lets things leak through. I felt that as surely as I felt my own heartbeat.

Edward lunged for me and pain outlined in his expression. I turned to buy myself more time and darted to the left, lifting my heels all the while. One-two-three, one-two-three. He grabbed again and I stepped backward, a bastardization of our wedding dance set to the consistent pattern of the numbers. One-two-three, one-two-three. So close. I ducked again to the left.

"I'm sorry, m'lady."

Morwood wrapped his big arms around me from behind and pinned my arms to my sides. I struggled, but there was no room to move. My head swam with beasts, pulsing in their unnatural gait, both too human and not human enough. They were near. So near. I drew my left leg up and tucked my knee as high as possible to block my abdomen. A futile move but all I could do.

"Please! You do not know what you are doing. Let me finish!"

"Dear Violet. I am so sorry."

I do not recall what happened next, only that the pressure and the crawling sensation had grown so intense that I had emptied the contents of my stomach there on the kitchen floor. I woke in my bed, restrained by the wrists and ankles. I twisted and tried to sit up but could not. I yelled for help, hoping that Beatrice might hear my pleas and release me before Edward or Morwood stopped her.

Alas, it was my Edward who came to me. That one unruly lock of his dark hair lay alone in the center of his forehead. His warm eyes welled with tears.

"My Violet. How I'd hoped he was wrong."

"Who? Let me go! You don't understand!"

He only nodded, as if not hearing me, with his mouth drawn into a thin line. "I should have listened to Greggson. I'd spent all those weeks apart from you, ignoring the signs he had foretold, moving about our finances. Had we more balsam, I could have brought in Dr. Thorogood from London, who specializes in the treatment of vapors such as these. Marwood kept an eye on you for me in secret whilst I tried. I failed you, my dear heart."

Edward wiped his eyes then drew one hand across my brow, his touch as gentle as ever. I recoiled from the man who had become my captor and strained against the ties that bound me.

"Edward. They are coming. I am the only one who can stop them."

"Dear Violet. I know you believe this madness to be true and I love you despite it. But look at you." He gestured at my arms, still raw from my scratches. "You've hurt yourself."

He blinked and one tear slid down his cheek. "You will only be kept away until the baby's birth to ensure its safety and yours, and then you will be returned here. To me. I promise you, then you will be free to live out your Banbury story and visit our son at your leisure."

"Daughter. We are having a daughter, not that you deigned to tell me so. They want to eliminate her before she can grow into her heritage and take my place as the keeper of the stones. They want to end my family line."

"So much like her mother, m'lord." Morwood stepped in from the shadows. "This affliction must pass through the blood."

"Yes, I am like Mother." A bit of hope sprung forth in my chest. "Did you know, Morwood? I am the lock, as she was before me. I am what stands between. Tell him."

Morwood looked at me, eyes filled with pity, and rage crushed all my other emotions. My feet were bound and could not be flush with the floor. I tried to lift my heels in succession anyway, but only gave myself a painful cramp in my leg as a result. I cried out, sobbing now. Something unseen tugged harder at the thread connecting us by my belly. By my baby. The gentle swell of my belly thrust outward and I pressed myself into the mattress and cried out.

"She's to be next! Our daughter, she's next, and they're coming for her! Don't you see?"

I sobbed openly with fury, unable to hide my face. Unwilling to spare them my feelings. The two men studied their shoes, uncomfortable with the situation they caused. Edward cleared his throat.

"Greggson has sent a carriage. You'll spend the rest of your time with child at a private sanatorium, where he will be awaiting your arrival. He assures me it is a kind place. Discreet. You'll be cared for by nuns until the baby comes and then returned here to my care. Won't that be nice?"

"I want to stay here. Bring the nuns here." Perhaps I could compromise.

The two men glanced at each other. With the barest flick of his eyebrow, Edward shocked me with his bald disdain for my pleas. Not only did he refuse to believe me, he was of the mind that I would hurt our child. My child. Those were not accusations born of love. And all the while, my love for him had been so pure. So naive. All the horse riding and picnics, our time together in the library where we ate fruit and shared our stories. I had poured out my heart to him about who I was and how I protected this world and he said he loved me.

He said he trusted me.

I'd assumed that had meant he'd believed me.

Their faces shifted and pulled, and behind their usual countenance I saw the beasts they'd become when the stones poured forth their poison. I needed to tap them, more now than ever before. The insistence writhed inside of me, squeezing my heart tight and making my breath stab my lungs with sharp icicles. My vision blurred at the edges. I counted in sets of five in my thoughts, hoping it would be enough to gather strength.

"Edward," I said, as steadily as I could manage. "Please, don't let this be the last for all these next months. I haven't been held by you for two fortnight. Please. I love you."

I pressed the backs of my hands against the wood of the bed to still their trembling lest they give away my fury. I needed to be untied, and I was willing to play pretend to get what I needed.

He pushed his unruly bit of hair back with the rest, and his face softened as the lock of hair fell again. I dropped my head.

"Edward, dear heart. I have been emotional and foolish. I understand and I trust in your judgment as both my husband and the Marquess of this land. I only ask, instead of these ties that hold me, could it be your arms?"

Edward nodded; tears once again gathered in his eyes. "Morwood, please leave us. Alert me when the carriage has arrived."

"Begging your pardon, m'lord—"

"Go. That is an order."

Ever the one to follow a directive, Morwood spun on his heel and left the room. The door clicked shut behind him. Edward untied my arms and I rubbed my raw, sore wrists. He turned back to me after freeing my legs and opened his mouth to say something. Perhaps it would have been an apology. Perhaps an admission of love. Perhaps to finally tell me in celebration that our love created a child who grew inside me.

Alas, in that same moment, I knew something else with raw certainty.

I kicked him in the throat as hard as I could manage and stopped his words. Mother had said, toward her end, that I needed to be ready to give everything of myself to protect this world.

"I loved you," I whispered. "I was a fool to think you'd understand."

Edward sputtered, and his warm eyes bulged from his reddened face. He wavered and turned toward the door, so I used one of the strips of fabric he'd tied me with to pull him back by the neck. I pulled and twisted it, and he fell against the bed, splayed like a dolly. I held the fabric tight at an angle, the right angle, above him. Life drained from his body in lines parallel to the strength that rushed into my own. When it was over, I tapped his stilled throat three times with my left pointer finger, then brushed that one lock off his forehead.

I pushed myself back toward the head of the bed, away from him. My face contorted and I cried, sadness mingled with powerful relief. The tugging at my belly had stopped as soon as the last of Edward's life had gone. One head of the household was right. Two was such a weak number.

I sobbed into the bed linens. Morwood burst through the door and ran behind Edward to free him from the cloth. I said nothing though I knew it was too late. Grief sat in my throat, swollen and raw. Morwood clawed at the cloth to untwist it and shook poor Edward's body with the effort. When Beatrice appeared in the doorway, I leapt from the bed and pointed at Morwood.

"He's killed him! Oh God help us!"

Beatrice screamed. I took her hand, and we ran for the front door of the manor with enough haste that I was not able to tap. The force of Edward's death stilled the stones so completely that it would not matter, but I recited the numbers in my mind to be sure. We dashed outside into the cold air where a crew of surly men had arrived in a carriage, no doubt to escort me to the madhouse to imprison me.

"The butler has killed the Lord of this house and has tried to frame me as a madwoman. Please arrest him, go! I command you as your Marchioness to capture him before harm befalls the rest of us!"

The men glanced among themselves, and in their pause, I straightened my spine and spoke with the authority passed to me through my family line. "Go, or I will have you arrested as accomplices."

They ran toward the manor and I slumped against the carriage, then placed a hand upon my belly, over the dear girl in there. What a hideous act of sacrifice, just as I knew now that Mother had done for me, all those years ago. Father hadn't fallen. She'd pushed him. I rubbed my belly and supposed it would be my daughter's fate as well, someday. I'd hoped Mother had been wrong about me, but isn't it always like children to think an outcome will be different for them?

Months later, I gathered my robe about my swollen belly and held the candlestick in my left hand. It was always my left. Down and down into the cellar, I followed the twisted lines to the stones. My daughter had been making her presence known for some time now, first fluttering then moving and kicking inside. How her father would have loved to lay his hand on the swell of my abdomen and talk to her. Grief flooded my senses, and I paused on the stair while the emotion swelled and passed. Along with it came a tightening of my belly. This would be my last time, alone in my family line. I continued on, despite the discomfort.

"Someday, my darling, this will be your burden to bear," I whispered, "and you will find your own ways to strengthen the lock. The one thing that remains a certainty is the numbers. No matter how the stones struggle and make you ill. You must touch the stones with the numbers."

Since Edward's death, the stones had quieted and coming here to tap them felt no different than remembering to tend my plants or return correspondence. I still performed the other tasks as they beckoned, but doing so no longer drained my body of energy. I had the physical strength to nurture the baby inside me. At the barest edges of my vision, I felt more than saw the beasts as they waited. Angry and hissing, but farther away. For now.

I transferred the candlestick to my right hand, passing it above the protruding belly where my daughter readied herself to meet me.

One, two, three, four, five.

I tapped my pattern in a set of thirteen and on the final tap, my belly tightened again, stronger this time. I smiled through the discomfort, and retraced my steps back up to the kitchens where I rang for Beatrice. The next in a long line of locks was on her way.

Horoscope for Puzzlers

Aquarius (Jan 20 - Feb 18): Believe in at least three impossible things before breakfast.

Pisces (Feb 19 - Mar 20): Shuffle the deck and draw something new.

Aries (Mar 21 - Apr 19): Grit your teeth and keep going. It won't seem so bad once it's done.

Taurus (Apr 20 - May 20): Manage your expectations sensibly and expect more from yourself.

Gemini (May 21 - Jun 20): Collaboration brings out the best in you, so make today a duet.

Cancer (Jun 21 - Jul 22): Life is short and your patience, shorter. Remember to breathe.

Leo (Jul 23 - Aug 22): Running from your problems will only make your calves cramp.

Virgo (Aug 23 - Sept 22): Pick up that hobby again and dare to play.

Libra (Sept 23 - Oct 22): Beware the dream of excess. It too will fade.

Scorpio (Oct 23 - Nov 21): Sometimes life needs a little fluff. Take the evening off.

Sagittarius (Nov 22 - Dec 21): Recall past events. They give insight to the present.

Capricorn (Dec 22 - Jan 19): You will meet a small, mysterious man. Feed him well.

A MODEL TOWN

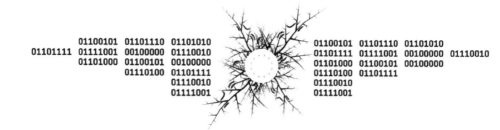

```
        01100101 01101110 01101010                    01100101 01101110 01101010
01101111 01111001 00100000 01110010                   01101111 01111001 00100000 01110010
        01101000 01100101 00100000                    01101000 01100101 00100000
                 01110100 01101111                    01110100 01101111
                          01110010                    01110010
                          01111001                    01111001
```

BY MARK MITCHELL

Another week in the books. Edwin pulled into the driveway and shut off the car's engine. He wiped his face with both hands, elbows on the steering wheel. Slanted sunlight came through a thin layer of grime that had built up over the week. Tomorrow would be Saturday, his day to wash the car and do some maintenance yard work. But right now what he really wanted was a good stiff drink.

He removed his hands from his face and looked out the driver's side window. The neighborhood was quiet. No one else out, but that had been the modus operandi around here for some time, and Edwin had no reason to desire a chance in that fact.

On the passenger seat sat his briefcase and hat. He grabbed his items and exited the vehicle. A breeze blew across the street, from one side to the other and then repeated every few seconds or so. Edwin at one time felt it was a strange phenomenon but figured it was the result of the layout of the houses that funneled certain winds to blow in a predictable direction. He squinted into the setting sun before following the footpath to the front door.

"Honey, I'm home," Edwin said upon entering the house. The smells of dinner permeated from out of the kitchen. Roast turkey with all the trimmings. The standard Friday night meal.

Edwin tossed his briefcase and hat into the chair by the record player. He picked an album at random and put it on the platter. The needle hissed as it began its travel around the vinyl record. Jazz music came from the speakers.

"Welcome home, dear," said Edwin's wife.

Marge wore a polka-dot dress, nude hosiery, and bright red high heels to match her lipstick and earrings. She wiped her hands on her apron as she crossed the room to deliver a kiss on Edwin's cheek.

"How was work?" she asked.

"Oh, the usual," Edwin sighed. He gave a wan smile. Marge cradled his face in her hand and returned a smile of her own.

"Anything noteworthy happen?"

"No." Edwin furrowed his brow. "Not that comes to mind. Actually, nothing comes to mind. Once I leave the house in the morning, it's all a blur until I come home."

She took his hand in hers and gave it a pat.

"My poor baby," she said. "You just need to put your feet up for a bit. Dinner will be ready soon. Can I get you a drink?"

"No thanks," Edwin said. "I'll do it myself." He crossed to the bar on the other side of the room. There were a few seconds of silence till the next song played on the record. "You want one?"

"A gin fizz," she said, "if you don't mind?"

A timer went off in the kitchen. She went running after it, taking small strides in her heels. The comical nature of her movement brought a more natural smile to Edwin's lips. He fixed the drinks and took hers to her in the kitchen before sitting down on the couch and taking off his shoes.

He sipped his scotch while he gazed, absently, about the room. It struck him funny how he saw the same things every day, but didn't really see them. Like artwork hanging on the walls you will pass by each day and never stop to appreciate.

They had the latest furniture designs—the salesman assured them these styles would be around for decades, though Edwin had been less than sure. Now that he studied their decor, he was certain the cream-colored couch and aquamarine carpeting were already dated. Not to mention the teak wood coffee table done in the Danish modern style and the chairs with their thin, peg legs. "Your house will feel light and airy, uncluttered," the salesman had said. "You'll feel like you're floating in a dream." Edwin scoffed and finished his drink.

The house had become anything but light and airy. Edwin felt choked by the standard design. It was like living in a Sears ad. He was sick of all the straight lines and open floor plan. Their house was a cookie-cutter version of the model home they'd toured before the neighborhood had been built. Lacking all individuality and a lived-in appearance. Edwin wanted a change.

He stood to make himself a second drink before dinner.

"Oh," Marge said from the kitchen. "I almost forgot. A package came for you today. I put it on the credenza in the hall for you."

Intrigue perked up in Edwin's ears. The package could only be one thing.

He put the stopper back into the neck of the scotch decanter. Ice cubes tinkled in his glass as he made his way around to the hall. Sitting on the credenza was an unassuming square parcel, but the sight of it lit up Edwin's features. He set his drink down and rummaged in the drawers for something to open the package with.

Using a dusty, forgotten corkscrew from the back of the bottom drawer, Edwin made quick work of the box and removed the surrounding brown paper from the item inside. He held up the miniature gas station to his eyes and smiled with a child's glee.

"It finally came," Edwin said as he entered the kitchen.

Marge removed a twelve-pound turkey from the oven and set it on the stovetop. Comical levels of steam came off the bird with the paper caps on the end of its legs. She removed her oven mitts and turned to see what Edwin had to show her.

"Isn't it a beaut?" Edwin beamed at her.

"Would you take a look at that," she said and stepped over to view the building closer. "That certainly is a beaut."

"I'm going to paint it so it matches Fremont's fill-up in town."

"Hey, that's going to be grand," she said.

"Uh-huh." He turned to leave.

"Wait, are you going now? Dinner's ready."

"Oh." Edwin paused in his retreat. He looked down at the gas station in his hands and then over to the turkey resting on the stove. "I was just going to…"

Marge untied her apron and hung it up. She grabbed Edwin by the hand and led him over to the table she had set while he'd been opening his parcel.

"There will be plenty of time," she said and helped him to his seat. "After you've had something to eat." She took the gas station from him and placed it aside, sure to keep it where he could see it. He had been waiting an awfully long time for it to arrive.

They ate dinner with the usual amount of conversation, town gossip, and compliments to the chef, though several times Marge had to urge Edwin to slow down and not shovel his food in. That would be a sure way to indigestion. He knew she was right, but he couldn't help himself. The gas station was one of the final pieces missing from his town.

In between bites of food he would flick his eyes over to make sure nothing had happened to his newest acquisition. The building patiently waited for Edwin to have his dessert—pistachio pudding—and a cup of coffee. Edwin wiped his mouth and stood. He gave Marge a kiss on the top of the head and snatched up the miniature gas station before proceeding down the hall to his studio.

The room he used for a studio had been intended to be a den or library by the tract developers, but the open space and shelves served his needs well for his hobbies. Along one wall were bottles of paint, the kind in tiny jars with silver tops, in every color imaginable. Next to them were cups with brushes sticking up; brushes with wide fans for general paints and some with delicate points used for precise detail.

Another wall had bottles of glue and miscellaneous items Edwin used to create things they didn't carry at the hobby store. With the mismatched items he could make his own trees or rolling hills with spring flowers always in bloom. He had an aggregate he used to make roads with. A bucket of nuts and bolts, and other pieces of metal to construct miniature telephone poles and antennas on the houses.

Really to call this a hobby would be inaccurate. No, for Edwin, managing his town was a way of life. It not only allowed him to blow off steam on the weekends, but perfecting every tiny detail was something he genuinely looked forward to. And nothing was more exciting than adding another structure to his model town.

The town itself sat in the middle of the room, in pride of place. Edwin had secured multiple card tables together to act as the mantle on which the town sprung up. Sections of plyboard was what the town actually stood on. A downtown area with a main street of shops stood in contrast to the neighborhood on the other side of the model. A near complete facsimile of Edwin's own in fact.

Edwin flipped the light switch as he entered his studio, and the lights above the town bathed the model in a warm yellow light. He held the gas station out for the town to see.

"Here it is, everyone," Edwin said to the model. "I told you it was coming."

He approached the town and laid the gas station in its proper place. He then took a step back to admire the whole scene. Arms akimbo, he surveyed his town with pride.

"Now everyone doesn't need to worry about running out of fuel again." He leaned over the neighborhood section, to a house that appeared just like his own. "Isn't that right, Edwin Jr.?"

He peered into the house where a man and his wife sat in the living room reading together. Parked outside the model home was a red and white corvette coup. He picked the car up and blew a layer of dust off the top.

"Let me fill 'er up and have her waxed for you," Edwin said. "No need to thank me."

He took the car over to his workbench and flipped on a small lamp. Edwin liked to keep his model clean and looking fresh, so on the workbench were rags, and more brushes drying from the last time he used them.

Giving the car a once-over with one of the rags, he had the car spotless in no time. Then he placed the car on the model and pushed it along with his forefinger, stopping at all the stop signs—no need to break the law, even in a pretend world—besides, who would you pay the imaginary ticket to? The car arrived at the gas station, the first customer of what would surely be many.

"Hmm," Edwin thought out loud. He scratched his chin. "I'll have to get a bell for when the cars pull up."

With the aid of his finger, the car returned home and Edwin backed the car into the driveway, opposite from the way it had been parked before. Now it was time to get to painting the gas station to match Fremont's.

Edwin turned on a small, portable radio on the workbench and tuned it into a baseball game being played on the other side of the country. He whistled as he perused his vast supply of paints, picking out the eggshell white and forest green, the color scheme of Fremont's.

He sat down on the stool before the workbench and slid a drawer from a toolbox. In the top drawer were a pair of magnifying glasses, which he perched on his nose and went about selecting the brushes he would need to use for the job at hand. Once everything had been selected, he dutifully worked at transforming the gas station. He took pride in his work, drawing the brush across the side of the building always in the same direction to give a uniform coat of paint. Once he had finished, Edwin removed the glasses from his face and sat still for a moment to appreciate his work.

He turned off the radio, which he had hardly listened to anyway, and flipped on a small desk fan and set it to oscillate across the workbench to help dry the paint on the gas station. The breeze blew across from one side of the bench to the other and back again.

Before calling it quits, Edwin wished the town a goodnight. He left the fan on, hoping to remember in the night to come turn it off. The lights he did turn off as he made his way to bed, where his wife was already sound asleep.

The next morning, groggy from uneven sleep, Edwin scooted his way down the hall. As he passed his studio, he remembered he hadn't turned the fan off in the middle of the night like he told himself to. Entering the room, however, he found himself more confused.

The fan was off, and the gas station had been positioned in its proper place within the model town.

Now how did that happen, Edwin thought. He must have done it while walking in his sleep. Marge wouldn't have done it; she knew better than to mess with his things—at least when it came to his hobbies. He frowned at the model town but pushed any more thought about it from his mind.

He shuffled into the kitchen and took a seat at the table. Marge wished him a good morning and slid a cup of coffee in front of him.

"Eggs and bacon, alright?" she asked.

"Grand," he said before blowing on his coffee.

He took a sip. Bitter and strong. Just as he liked it. He set the mug down.

"You didn't by any chance turn off the fan in my studio this morning, did you?"

Marge stood at the counter, buttering some toast. She put the toast on a plate and brought it to the table.

"No," she said. "You know I don't go in there, except to vacuum."

"Strangest thing." Edwin pulled the plate of toast closer. "Guess I must have done it then." He stared at the toast in his hand. Marge set down the eggs and bacon. She placed her arms akimbo.

"You feeling okay?"

Edwin broke his stare and found his wife looking at him, worried.

"Fine," he said. "A little tired is all."

She went about her business before joining him at the table. They ate their breakfast together, swapping pages of the newspaper as each finished reading from the various sections. With breakfast over, and him feeling more awake, Edwin set to do his weekend chores.

He grabbed the bucket and wash mitt from the garage and made his way out to the driveway. Next, he unraveled the hose and brought it over to his car. Right before he began to wet it down, he stopped, surprised for the second time that morning.

Not only had his car been reversed from how he parked it when he arrived home from work, but the grime and dust on the windows had been removed. The car was spotless.

Edwin took a step back and scratched his head.

"Well, how do you like that."

Turning off a desk fan and moving the gas station, that was something he could believe he'd do in his sleep, but washing the car in the middle of the night? He couldn't have done that, not without Marge noticing and asking him about it this morning.

Just as he was contemplating calling the doctor to look into his nocturnal behaviors, a voice called out to him from across the street.

"Morning neighbor!"

Edwin looked up at a man standing with a hose in one hand, the other up in the air waving at him. The man wore a loud Hawaiian shirt and khaki pants. He smiled at Edwin almost as brightly as his shirt.

"Morning," Edwin said, automatically. The truth was he had never seen the man before in his life. This was about the last straw. The fan, the car, and now new neighbors? He thought he needed to go back to bed and lay down.

"Beautiful day, huh?"

"You bet," Edwin said as he collected the car detailing tools he no longer needed. He stopped and furrowed his brow. "I'm sorry, I'm having kind of a strange morning...have we met before?"

"Where are my manners?" The man shut off his hose and dropped it on the lawn to walk over. He led with a damp hand. "Name's Harold. Me and the misses just moved in. We haven't had a chance to introduce ourselves yet."

Finally some sanity. Edwin shook his hand.

"I'm Edwin. My wife, Marge, is just inside. I can go grab her—"

"No trouble," Harold said. "I'm sure we'll see more of each other." He pointed to his own house. "After all, we're neighbors now."

"Yeah," Edwin heard himself say.

"I can see you're busy, I'll let you get to it. Nice to meet you."

"Same."

Harold trotted across the street and picked up his hose to resume watering his already vibrant green lawn.

Edwin scooped up the remaining bucket and mitt and headed back inside. From across the street, Harold waved at him.

Marge was in the kitchen preparing tuna fish sandwiches for lunch when Edwin came in.

"I met the new neighbor," he said. He turned on the faucet to wash his hands, though they hadn't had the chance to get dirty. Marge looked over at him.

"New neighbors?"

"Yeah, Harold…" Edwin paused. "I didn't catch a last name. Anyway he seems nice enough. He mentioned a wife, though I didn't meet her." He dried his hands off on the dish towel. "Do you know when they moved in? I didn't hear any trucks or anything."

Marge folded the sandwiches closed and cut them diagonally.

"No," she said, "not that I noticed either."

They sat and ate. Edwin told her about the car and his concern he may have developed a midnight exercise program, walking around in his sleep. She doubted it, but listened to him and offered a few words of comfort. With the meal over, Marge said she had a couple errands to run and inquired whether or not he would like to join. He declined, saying he would spend some time in his studio.

Edwin watched his wife drive off before going to gaze upon his model town. He dug in one of his drawers in the toolbox that contained miscellaneous items and pulled out a figure of a man. The man would be a suitable stand-in for his new neighbor, Harold.

The shirt he painted yellow and red. The pants got a coating of tan. Then once dried, Edwin placed the figurine in the model, across the street from the replica of his house.

"Welcome to the neighborhood, Harold."

Thirst overcame him and Edwin craved a beer from the icebox. He pushed himself away from the model to leave when something caught his eye. It couldn't be. Is that a…?

Edwin bent down and picked up a small white square from the front porch of his model home. There appeared to be some writing on the small box, so he retrieved his magnifying glasses from the workbench. Lo and behold, an inscription was made out as if the package had been delivered from some toy store in Poughkeepsie.

He set the package down, wondering if he should open it. Where could it have come from? It seemed someone was playing a joke on him, but who? Certainly not Marge, but no one else came into his house. That he knew of.

Instead of opening the package, Edwin removed the roof of the house and peered inside. Miniature versions of his own furniture were scattered throughout the model, or at least they closely resembled his own things. He moved over the model until he got to where the fake studio would be. A gasp escaped from his mouth.

His fake self had started his own model town.

Curiosity won out and Edwin used a pair of tweezers to open the tiny package. Inside was a small building. Not a gas station, thank goodness, that would have been too weird—as if these events weren't weird already—no, inside the package was a post office.

Edwin dropped everything and backed away. He didn't know why, but he was suddenly afraid of his model town. Stumbling down the hall, he made his way to the kitchen and that beer waiting in the fridge.

He downed more than half the bottle in one pull, wiping the foam from his lips with the back of his hand. Across the street he spied Harold still watering his lawn.

Stars circled around Edwin's head. He had to sit. Nothing made any sense. He had to know what was going on but didn't know how to start to make heads or tails out of it all.

The sun had set by the time Marge returned home from her errands. She flipped the light switch to find Edwin sitting in the dark at the kitchen table.

"Oh, Edwin! You gave me quite a start," she said and held a hand over her fluttering heart. He stood and took hold of her arm.

"Come here," he said. "I have to show you something."

"Can't it wait," she said. "I have ice cream to get into the freezer before it further melts."

He simply said, "No."

He led her down the hall and they stood in the entryway of the studio.

"Well?"

"Am I supposed to see something?" she asked.

"You don't hear it?" Edwin led her closer to the model.

"Hear what?"

"Listen." Edwin held a finger to his lips. He cocked his head at an angle. A smile spread across his face. "Do you hear it?"

"Sounds like a radio or something turned way down low," she said. "May I go now?"

Before she could turn to leave, Edwin popped the roof of his model home. In the living room two figurines sat on the couch watching tv. The miniature tv emitted a soft glow from the black and white picture. It was hard to make out, but looked like they were watching a sitcom show.

"Hey," Marge said, coming closer. "That's something. Where did you get a small tv like that? How does it work?"

"I didn't get it," Edwin said and waited for the follow-up he knew would come.

"What do you mean you didn't get it?"

"It just showed up. Kind of like Harold across the street." Edwin walked around to the other side of the model town. "I can't explain it, but something weird is going on."

Marge stood up and laughed.

"Edwin, if you're pulling my leg—"

"I'm not. I swear."

She looked over at him. His face gave no indication of mirth.

"He even built himself a studio. Like this room we're in." Edwin pointed to the small studio. "They've come to life or something." He picked up his figurine and examined it.

"They're moving on their own now."

"You expect me to believe it?"

"I don't even believe it," Edwin said. "But it's true. He got this small package delivered today."

Edwin handed her the small white box with the tiny post office inside. Marge moved it up to her face and then rolled her eyes over to Edwin. She smiled and handed it back.

"Enough, Edwin." She turned on her heels. "I have groceries to put away and dinner to start." She walked out of the room. Edwin followed.

"I swear I'm not making this up," he continued.

"You've seen them moving?" Marge unpacked the brown paper bags in the kitchen and began to put the items away.

"Well, no. Not physically." Edwin searched the room for an explanation. "But they are moving, how else would you explain how they got a television set? I don't think they sell those at the hobby store. Certainly not working ones."

"I can't explain that," she said and put a loaf of bread away in the bread box. She turned around and let out a breath, giving him a sorrowful look.

"What?"

"You're making me worried," she said. "I'm going to my mother's house to-morrow, as you know. I think you should come with me."

"Why, so you can keep an eye on me?"

"That," she said, taking a head of lettuce from the brown bag, "and I think it would do you some good. Get away for a while. See something different."

"I'm not crazy," he said. He moved over to the window. Harold was watering his lawn across the street. Did he ever go inside?

"I didn't say that, Ed."

"But you're thinking it." He held up his hand before she could utter a rebuttal. "I'll be fine, okay? I won't even go near the model tomorrow."

She watched him go out of the kitchen.

He went down the hall and stood in the entryway to his studio and wondered what the people of his model town had been up to behind his back this time. It seemed the model town was somehow connected with his own world. What happened in one affected the other, as strange as that sounded. To test his theory, he picked up the model of his own home and rotated it forty-five degrees.

"There," he said. "That should prove I'm not losing my mind."

Even before the words left his lips, he doubted them. Perhaps that was the only explanation for what was going on.

The next morning the sun beat through the windows facing their bed, waking Edwin with blinding light. He sat up and held a hand to the harsh rays.

"What the hell?"

He swung his legs out and crept to the window. The window, which Edwin had been certain always faced south, now held the sun in all its glory, rising in the East.

Marge stretched behind him and yawned.

"Ah, what a glorious morning," she said. "It's always so nice waking to the warmth of the sun. How'd you sleep, dear?"

Edwin turned from the window, puzzlement all over his countenance.

He said, "The sun's never shown like this first thing in the morning."

Marge shrugged into her robe and tied it at the waist. She murmured a "Hmmm?"

"The window," Edwin said. "It used to face the other way, didn't it?"

She smiled at him and patted his hand. "I'll go start the coffee." She gave him a peck on the cheek as she passed out of the room.

Edwin went back to the window for a second look. This was all wrong. He knew it in his heart. This had never been the view from their bedroom.

He ran out the front door and down the driveway, which now had a swoop to it, as opposed to the straight angle he remembered. He stood in the middle of the lawn and gazed at his house. The whole structure had moved the forty-five degrees he'd turned the model the night before.

"That's not possible…"

"Morning neighbor!"

Edwin turned to the source. Harold watering his lawn in his bright Hawaiian shirt. Harold waved, to which Edwin gave a hasty wave back before going back inside.

He checked the model. Sure enough it was positioned as he had turned it, but now it had a matching swoop of a driveway painted onto the plyboard.

"No," Edwin said, fear in his voice. "No, this can't be happening."

"Oh there you are." Marge entered the studio, putting on her earrings. "I've been looking for you. My mother called and asked if I could come early, so you'll have to make your own breakfast."

Edwin didn't look at her but kept his focus on the model.

"Did you hear me?" She moved to get within his vision. "I thought you said you wouldn't go near the model today?"

He had a wide-eyed frown on his face.

"Are you alright?" she asked.

Edwin didn't respond.

"Well," she said. "I'll check in on you later. Call if you need anything."

She lingered for a moment to see if he would respond. But when he didn't, she left. The sound of the car starting came muffled through the wall.

Edwin stared at the car in the driveway of the model, fully expecting to see it move on its own. Outside his house, his wife pulled out of the driveway and the sound of the car's engine grew fainter and fainter as she drove off.

Thankfully the model's car didn't move.

He let out his breath and relaxed for the first time that morning. Maybe he wasn't slipping as much as he feared, but he still couldn't explain all the weird things he'd been seeing that weekend.

"Get a grip, Edwin," he said to himself. He closed his eyes and took a few calming deep breaths, but when he opened them, his heart began to pound.

The model car had vanished.

A notion to take the roof off of the model house compelled him to do so. Inside he found his own figurine sitting on the couch, covering his face with his hands. Nowhere could he find the figurine for his wife.

Edwin picked up the miniature version of himself and attempted to pry the hands from the face. Of course he couldn't do it. The figurine was made from cast-iron; nothing could move it without the heat of a blazing fire.

A sadness overtook Edwin.

He flung the figure across the room. Tears filled his eyes and his face burned with anger. He searched the room for a sturdy object to enact his frustrations with.

When he didn't find anything to suit his needs, he ripped the rod from the closet, spilling their winter coats and little used garments to the floor.

Edwin stepped up to the model and smacked the wooden rod against his palm. He had spent countless hours and days on the model. Many of his happiest times over the course of the past couple years had been working on the model. Only two days ago he had been over the moon to receive the gas station, the final piece to his model. It had been completed, finally. Edwin's heart had overflowed with joy and accomplishment. Now looking at the model made his stomach churn.

He despised the model town.

Lifting the rod over his head, Edwin brought it down with force. Splinters of the model flew in all directions. He swung again. And again. And again.

He gritted his teeth and yelled obscenities as he brought destruction to the town. What had taken months to build, only took moments to annihilate.

The vicious blows broke down the buildings into smaller and smaller pieces, until they could no longer be discerned for what they used to be.

Edwin stopped and rested. The exertion had winded him. Sweat broke out on his brow and ran down his flushed cheeks. The town was obliterated.

"There," he said. "It's done."

He didn't really believe these words, though he wished them to be true. He waited through the brittle silence to see if his own world would be affected by the changes brought on to the model town.

When nothing occurred, he slumped against the wall and slid to a seated position. Something dug into the underside of his thigh and he leaned over to remove the offending shrapnel.

He held up his figurine. The one that had been crying within the model home. Somehow in all the chaos it had wound up along the wall. Edwin was about to toss it aside, when he noticed the figurine no longer had his hands in front of his face, but instead it held them out in front of him. A terrified expression upon the face.

Frightened by the change in the cast-iron man, Edwin dropped the figurine and brought up the wooden rod again. He stood over the little man.

"Enough," he yelled. Spittal flew from his mouth. "Enough, now."

Whatever energy and anger he had left in him, Edwin transferred through the closet rod onto the cast-iron figurine. The miniature man bounced with every impact, some of which didn't even come in contact with him, but instead landed on the floor. The carpet beneath Edwin's feet shifted and tore. Still he kept up his brutal assault until his arms grew heavy and he could no longer lift the rod.

The wooden pole made a dull sound against the bunched up carpeting when Edwin let it go from his grasp. Newsprint poked through the holes in the carpet.

Edwin tilted his head at the strange sight.

He dropped to his knees and tore the carpet away. Underneath lay a newspaper, albeit one big enough to cover the whole room and then some. The letters on the paper were twice the size of his own hand.

Gasping, Edwin stood and backed away to get a bigger picture of what he was seeing.

Along the top of the section of newspaper visible to him was a date: January 20th, 2004.

A pang gripped his stomach and Edwin suddenly felt dizzy. How could a newspaper, the largest he'd ever seen, and from the future no less, have gotten under his carpet? His house had been built almost sixty years prior to the date indicated. It just wasn't possible.

Edwin had the urge to run to the phone and call his wife. She must have arrived at her mother's by now. Perhaps he could ask her to come home. He needed someone else to see what he saw, to verify he hadn't made it all up in his mind. Then music began to play.

He knew it wasn't coming from inside the house, because the music had a strange, dissonant quality to it. It both sounded far away but booming at the same time. That's when he realized it was coming out of the sky.

What else could shock him today, he wondered.

Edwin was about to run to the window and throw up the sash when the entire room was engulfed in darkness. As if something had blotted out the sun. A coldness crept over him and stilled his movements. In fact, he couldn't move at all, even if he wanted to. Fear impaired his motor functions. His mouth went dry. He wanted to scream, but nothing would come out.

The darkness moved across the room. It had been a shadow of something large outside his house. And now it came closer.

The roof cracked and light flooded the room. A hand reached in and wrapped around Edwin. The strength of the giant hand could have crushed him if it chose to.

Wind rushed past Edwin's face as he was lifted out of the home. All at once he saw behind him a model town, his home a small version of the expansive room now around him.

The hand turned him around and Edwin stared into the eyes of a giant man. A man who looked very much like himself.

Edwin's limbs felt a tremendous weight and he found he couldn't move, not even to blink. It was as if his arms and legs were made of cast-iron.

Once in a while, I have a nagging feeling about something. Maybe a bit of song, or a scent I've picked up, or some other tiny piece of a memory that I cannot place. Usually I have to just let it go, because I can't google my brain.

If only life had a table of contents.

That thing, that little broken-off piece of a thorn, gets stuck sometimes and I get so focused on it. I can't let it go, but all it does is fester until I have to forcibly pry it out of my mind if I can't place the bit of memory.

Sometimes though, I can. That feeling of finding where it fits, of understanding the context of that teeny-tiny little nagging thought, feels as satisfying as the cool side of your pillow on a warm night. Of straightening a bunched-up sock inside your shoe. Of having exactly the right number of buns for the burgers at your picnic.

One time, years ago, a cleanser used at a hospital where I worked had this sharp citrus smell to it. Not lemon, like a typical cleanser. Something sweeter. Slightly fruity. Something with a chemical undertone that said, "this smells tasty, but nothing about it is natural."

Every few weeks or so, I'd catch a whiff of the smell but could not place it. A year of this went by. I'd tried to explain it to family and friends, tried to find the smell in other areas of my life, hoping to stumble into the memory in real time. All to no avail.

Then one day, the smell lingered once again in the hallway, and the right log wiggled loose in the river of my memories. That smell reminded me of the original Tart 'N' Tinys, sold by Wonka in the 1980s and discontinued in the 1990s. Was the smell of the cleanser even the same as the candy? Probably not. Something in my mind linked the two together, though, and once the mystery had been solved, I felt a profound sense of satisfaction. The thorn had finally been removed.

Gentle-reader, I hope you experience that same feeling with each puzzle you solve in this book, leading to the ultimate satisfaction: unlocked the final special feature. And if you ever happen upon some original Tart 'N' Tinys on a dusty, forgotten shelf, give them a sniff for me.

THE SQUATCH

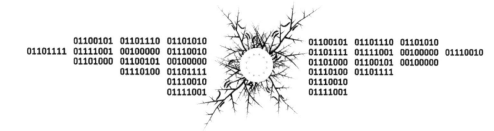

01100101 01101110 01101010
01101111 01111001 00100000 01110010
01101000 01100101 00100000
01110100 01101111
01110010
01111001

01100101 01101110 01101010
01101111 01111001 00100000 01110010
01101000 01100101 00100000
01110100 01101111
01110010
01111001

BY MARCEL LEROUX

They enter the campsite in a clump. Four of them. No tactics. No muzzle discipline. Lines of fire a spiderweb. A single grenade or machine-gun burst would take them all out.

They're not worried about that. Confident in their numbers. Their numbers and their hardware.

They come armed. Guns pressed to shoulders, shiny black barrels extended like insect antennae. One carries an assault rifle, festooned with add-ons and doodads. A conversation piece. Another holds a chrome revolver, two-handed, three-point stance. The leader.

Top half of his head is bald as a honeydew. Lower half a cloud of gray fur. A pink hole appears in the gray and sprays an innocent fern with brown glop. Same hole he barks orders out of.

"Spread out, you knuckleheads. Looks like we just missed him."

They wander around the site. Purposeful but directionless, like termites on a log. The one with the assault rifle reports back.

"Ain't here, Tuck."

"I can see that, Billy. You find anything tells us where he mighta gone to?"

"Me?"

"One I'm talking to, ain't you?"

Billy's younger than the rest. Hair shaved up the sides. Just a blond divot on top. Tattoo over his right eyebrow. Two words. Gothic script.

NO REGERTS

Billy looks to his older compatriots for support. They shrug. Lower their long guns. Disappointed. The hunt's over before it started.

One, a skinny gent with the gut of a man twice his size, says, "I don't see no tracks, Tuck. Coulda up and flew away for all we know."

He's got a hunting rifle. Bolt action. Old school. His vest is the color of a traffic cone. Visible from space on a clear day.

Tuck drenches that fern again and says, "Goddammit, you guys. He couldn't have got far. The fire's still burning. Look here. He's got a pot of Dinty Moore on. Still simmering. Ain't even burnt."

One with the shotgun says, "What you want us to do, Tuck?"

"What do I *want*? What I want is I *want* you to get your thumbs out of your bootyholes and get looking for this sonofabitch before he gets away. That's what I *want*."

They look at each other. Commiserate. *This* asshole.

They re-shoulder their weapons and head back into the woods. The dark swallows them instantly. The sound of their footsteps takes longer to fade.

I wait until the crickets start up again before I climb down out of the tree and finish my dinner.

I heard them coming a mile away. I mean that literally. Nobody camps out here. Not this far out. It's not forbidden but it is highly discouraged. I learned that from some hikers I met at a rest stop a hundred miles back. They gave me a lift and some good directions. I went in deeper than they recommended, marking landmarks on the way. Found a little spot, close enough to a brook I could follow downstream to civilization if I got turned around.

I like quiet. It's hard to find but worth the effort.

Been here two nights. No luck fishing, so tonight I broke out the Dinty Moore. It was bubbling up nice when I heard them coming, crashing and jibbering, snapping every twig from here to Portland. Maine *or* Oregon.

Not in the mood to entertain visitors, I made like a squirrel. There was no reason for anyone to be looking for me, not here, and certainly not these yokels, but I never explain when I can evade. Information is ammunition, and I don't hand that out for free.

Now I'm scraping the last of the stew off the pot, scarfing down every last calorie I can muster, when I hear them coming back my way. I wipe down the pot so it won't crust over and climb back into my tree.

They come stomping back in, grumbling. Weapons held low, practically dragging in the dirt.

Shotgun says, "Dinty Moore's gone." He pulls a pack of gas station cigarillos out of his breast pocket and fires one up. It smells like burning socks.

Billy says, "Maybe a coon got at it."

Tuck says, "Maybe."

He spits in the pot. I get an urge to scrub it out with his beard.

Orange Vest says, "Probably not even the guy."

"Not the guy, why's he hiding?" says Tuck.

"Maybe he's not hiding," says Billy. "Maybe—"

"Don't," says Tuck.

"Don't what?"

"Don't say what you're gonna say."

"How do you know what I'm gonna say?"

"You're gonna say maybe the squatch got him."

"Well, maybe he did."

"Goddammit, I said don't."

"I'm just sayin'."

"Give it a rest, Billy," says Orange Vest.

"But what about what Doc Pendleton said?"

Tuck says, "Doc Pendleton's a country veterinarian. Just because he can't identify a hair don't make it a bigfoot. Just means it ain't a dog or a cow."

"He said it looked like some kinda primate."

"Your mama looks like some kinda primate," says Orange Vest.

"I just don't think a man coulda done that to them campers."

"We don't know *what* a man done to them campers. Not after the coyotes got at 'em."

"Wasn't all coyotes."

"How do you know?"

"I heard things. My cousin, his baby-mama works in the county morgue."

"Doing what?"

"I don't know. Answering phones, I guess."

"So that makes your cousin's baby-mama an expert, huh? A whatchacallit, a pathologist?"

"No, but—"

"But nothing," says Tuck. "There's a man out here. A strange man don't no-body know nothing about, out here where nobody's supposed to be, and he's here the same night my sister's boy goes off with some out-of-staters and don't come back? My sister sitting at home, worried sick, and you're here yapping about a goddamn sasquatch? Don't you see how offensive that is?"

"I'm sorry, Tuck. I didn't mean to offend you."

"Well, you did. You did offend me."

"I said I'm sorry. I just—"

"You just what?"

"I just... Maybe there's a man out here—"

"There's a man out here. You think Bigfoot out here cooking Dinty Moore?"

"Okay, so there's a man out here. And maybe he even knows something. But he wasn't here last month when those campers got killed."

"How do we know that? Maybe he's been here a year, since them other hikers went missing, them girls, ones from California, and Randy here just didn't happen to notice his campfire smoke until last night."

"Yeah. Maybe. But what if, you know, what if it's all connected? What if the reason we can't find no tracks is because the squatch came and took this man right here where we're standing? Just came up on him while he's cooking his Dinty Moore and yoked him right up?"

"If he did, then where's the squatch tracks, them big-ass feet of his?" says Tuck.

"Squatch don't normally leave tracks, less the soil is particularly soft. That's why he's got them big feet to begin with. They're like snowshoes. Spread the body weight out."

"That's ridiculous. You're ridiculous. We've been living in these woods our whole lives. You ever seen a squatch? Randy, you ever seen a squatch?"

Orange Vest says, "'Sides Billy's mama? Never."

Shotgun says, "I seen a squatch once."

Crickets.

Tuck says, "You seen a squatch?"

"Once. When I was a boy."

"Bullshit."

"Says you."

Billy says, "What'd he look like?"

"Didn't get a real good look. Me and my daddy was out hunting. He bagged him a buck, a real beauty. 12-pointer. He's cleaning him, and I don't like watching that. Never could stand the smell of offal. So I've got my back turned, looking out into the woods, trying to hold my milk and cookies down. And then I see him, just cresting over top of a hill. More a shape than anything else. Like a man, but not a man. Too big for a man, but walking like a man. I only see him for a second, and then he's gone. Fast. Too fast to see him move. He's just there one second and then *poof*. Gone."

"Coulda been anything, Hurd," says Randy. "Coulda been a bear. A moose."

"You ever see any moose around here?"

"No, but I sure as shit ain't seen no squatch either."

Hurd says, "I know what I seen."

More crickets.

They get comfy. Cigarettes join Randy's cigarillo. Billy starts vaping from a plastic pen. Tuck pulls up the log I'd been using as a chair and flicks ashes into the fire.

Billy says, "How long we gotta wait here?"

Tuck says, "Till he comes back."

"What if he don't come back? Can't we just tell the sheriff we found his camp-site and let him take care of it?"

"Kimbrough ain't gonna do shit, and you know it. He told us as much. Far as the sheriff's office is concerned, the official position is there ain't no serial killer work-ing these woods, just inexperienced campers getting lost, succumbing to the elements and getting devoured by wildlife. Which makes it a parks department problem, and they ain't too eager to make a big deal out of it and scare off all the hikers who buy all the goddamn snow globes and bumper stickers in all the goddamn souvenir shops. You think if we could count on ol' Kimbrough to do a damn thing, we'd be up here getting eaten alive by mosquitos stead of sitting at home watching *Dancing With the Stars*?"

Randy says, "You watch *Dancing With the Stars*?"

"Well, the wife likes it."

"Oh sure. The wife."

"Look, I was skeptical at first, but you gotta admire the athleticism of some of these—"

Hurd says, "Shut up. You hear that?"

Billy says, "Hear what? I don't hear nothing."

"Shut up for a second and you will."

Randy says, "I hear it. It's like a creaking sound. Where's it coming from?"

Tuck says, "I don't know, but it's getting louder."

Billy jumps up and grabs that pimped-out assault rifle of his. He pans it around the perimeter of the campsite, nervousness making the barrel bob around like the fickle finger of fate. Right about then it seems to hit him how little of the darkness the camp-fire light reaches. The skin on his face seems to peel back, his eyes bulging out round and white as eggs, trying to peer into all that devouring black, wanting but *not* wanting to see the squatch of his nightmares coming for him.

He swings that gun around in parabolic arc, making his cohorts duck and curse.

"Billy, for Christ's sake, calm down!" yells Tuck, belly-first in the dirt. "It's probably just a squirrel!"

"Yeah, Billy, a squirrel! It's just a squirrel!" says Randy, also cowering, clutching his rifle to his orange vest like a prized teddy bear.

"A squirrel? At night? Squirrels don't come out at night!

"Maybe it's a night squirrel!"

"Squirrels are diurnal creatures! There ain't no night squirrel! THERE AIN'T NO NIGHT SQUIRREL!"

Hurd, the largest of the quartet, comes up behind him and scoops him up in a bear hug. Billy screams and squirts off a volley of automatic fire over Randy and Tuck's heads. The forest swallows up the bullets as easily as it does the firelight.

Now everybody's screaming. Billy mashes that trigger like he's playing *Call of Duty* on infinite ammo. It only takes a few seconds for the clip to run dry but it feels much longer. When the gunfire stops, so does the screaming. The silence is sudden and oppressive. Even the crickets hold off, waiting to see what happens next.

The only sound is a whole lot of breathing.

And that creaking again.

"It's just a branch or something," says Tuck, sitting up and brushing debris out of his beard. "Just a branch."

"But what's moving it?" says Billy, still in Hurd's arms, now hanging limp and heavy as a wet towel. "What's moving it?"

The answer is me. I'm what's moving it. They figure that out when the tree limb I'm on finally finishes snapping before I can move to a stronger one.

I drop hard and fast into their midst. I break some more branches on the way down, but they don't slow me much. I hit the ground heavy as a sandbag, sending up a puff of dirt and dried leaves.

They scream in four-part harmony. Billy provides percussion by clicking impotently at that empty trigger.

I say, "Ow."

Tuck pulls his big shiny revolver out of its holster and aims it casually at my face. The hole at the end looks like the Lincoln Tunnel.

"Well, well, well," he says. "And who might you be?"

I try to talk but the fall stole all my wind. My lungs are full of hot fiberglass. I try again and just cough for about a minute straight. When I can breathe again, I look him dead in the eye between the sights of that hand cannon, which I can now tell from my privileged vantage point is a .357 Taurus Model 66, which boasts an unusual seven-shot cylinder, just in case the first six don't do the job.

At this range, that's a half-dozen more than he'll need.

I clear my throat, spit out a wad of phlegm, and say, "They call me the Night Squirrel."

They zip-tie my hands behind my back, sit me down on my sitting log, and ask me some questions. Who am I? What am I doing here? Where's Trevor? A lot of that last one.

I tell them I'm just a hiker. That sounds better than the truth. "Drifter" has a negative ring to it. It's too close to "vagrant." They got laws against that sort of thing.

They accept that. They get lots of hikers around here. When I tell them I don't know any Trevor, though, they are less receptive.

They work me over a little. Tuck does the heavy lifting. I don't fight back and I don't shit-talk. Most men don't have it in them to really whale on a helpless person. You have to be a bad man to go through with something like that. And these aren't bad men. They aren't *great*, but they aren't *bad*.

I've been hit by bad men before. Bad men throw their whole heart and soul into it. This is nothing in comparison.

Honestly, the tree hit harder.

They mostly work the body. I engage the core and take it. I'll walk away with lots of bruising and no internal damage. When Tuck throws one tentative right at the face, I clench my jaw and brace my tongue against the roof of my mouth. Reduces the chance of a broken jaw. Plus. it stiffens the neck muscles, which lessens the kind of whiplash movement that makes the brain slosh around inside the skull. That's how you get concussed.

I *hate* getting concussed.

A few more punches and the old guy's tuckered out. He doesn't bloody my nose or loosen any teeth, which I appreciate.

Tuck's breathing heavy. He shakes his punching hand like he's putting out a match.

"Forget it," he says. "We'll take him into town. Let Kimbrough sweat it out of him."

"Are you kidding?" says Randy. "It's a five-mile hike back to Hurd's truck. In the dark? Why don't we just camp here for the night and leave first thing in the morning?"

"Oh hell no," says Billy. "I ain't staying out here. No way."

"What're you afraid of?" says Tuck. "We got the guy."

"Him? What is he, five-six? You think this little guy killed all those people?"

"Could be a lunatic," says Hurd. "Lunatics get that crazy lunatic strength."

"And what about the primate hair?"

"He's a primate, ain't he?"

"That's enough," says Tuck. "Maybe he's the guy, maybe he's not the guy. That's for the law to decide. But I for one am not staying out here sleeping on the cold ground with my back acting up when I got a nice, warm bed at home. Randy, you can stay here if you want but I am getting my ass back to town."

"Me too," says Billy.

"Hurd?"

"Don't matter to me either way. You want to hike, I'll hike."

"Well, I ain't staying out here by myself," says Randy.

"Then we'd better get a move on, huh?"

We move single file through the woods. Billy, Tuck, and Randy hold flash-lights, their guns holstered or hung on shoulder straps. Hurd takes the rear, his shotgun leveled at my spine in case I get any big ideas. Billy's in front of me, Tuck ahead of him, Randy leading the way.

It's slow going. The underbrush crunches under our boots.

"I don't like it out here," says Billy. "I ain't never been this far out before, and now I know why."

"It's just stories, Billy," says Randy. "You don't really think there's anything out here, do you? The real reason nobody comes out here is there's no trails. Easy to get turned around. You get lost, tree cover's so dense rescue choppers can't see in. So parents tell kids there's a bigfoot out here to keep 'em safe. That's all there is to it."

"What about what Hurd saw?"

"Hurd was just messing with you. Wasn't you, Hurd?"

Hurd says, "No comment."

Billy says, "And he wasn't the only one. Everybody knows somebody who knows somebody who got a squatch story."

"People tell stories for all kinds of reasons," says Tuck. "My wife's mother's sister used to say the archangel Gabriel appeared to her and told her to divorce her husband and open up a fabrics store. It was a lot easier than admitting she kicked him out cuz he knocked up their seventeen-year-old babysitter."

"I'm just saying," says Billy. "I don't care if it's a sasquatch or a wendigo or ancient Indian spirits or what. The vibes are wrong out here. These are bad woods. That's all there is to it."

I stop walking. Hurd's shotgun pokes me in the back.

"Keep it moving," he says.

I say, "Shhh."

"Don't you shhh me."

"Listen."

"Why should I listen to you?"

"Not to me."

Hurd gives his ear a courtesy cock and says, "I don't hear anything."

"It's stopped."

"Convenient. Look, pal, you ain't fooling me. I know there ain't no night squirrel."

He prods me with the shotgun. I resume walking. The noises start up again, timed to our footsteps. You have to be listening to notice them. We crunch, they crunch. It goes like that for another quarter mile.

Then they stop.

I halt again, expecting to get another prod in the back. But there's nothing. I turn around.

No Hurd.

I say, "Um…"

The others don't notice anything. They keep walking, cones of light bobbing up and down.

The crunching starts up again, keeping pace with their steps.

I could just let them go. Sneak off into the dark. Lay low. Let them draw off whoever's out there. Wait for dawn. Pack up my gear. Get back on the road.

Forget I was ever here.

I think about it for a second longer than I'm proud of. I should just leave them to their fate, but I can't.

Like I said, they're not bad men.

"Guys," I say. "I think we have a situation."

They stop. Turn around. Shine their flashlights in my face, blinding me. Their voices come at me from a white haze.

Billy says, "Where's Hurd?

Tuck says, "Yeah, what'd you do with Hurd?"

Randy says, "Hurd! Come on out! Stop messing around!"

I say, "There's someone else out here."

Billy says, "I knew it!" He joins Randy in calling Hurd's name.

Tuck says, "Bullshit! What'd you do to him?"

"Me? I got my hands zip-tied behind my back. What do you think I am, a ninja?"

"Maybe! You coulda done some kickboxing shit!"

"Then why wouldn't I just try to get away?"

"I don't know! Maybe you got some kinda nefarious scheme!"

"Would you please get that light out of my face?"

"No! I'm onto you, asshole! Start talkin'!"

I turn my head and blink away the haze. It occurs to me that now there's only one voice calling for Hurd.

When my vision clears, Randy's not there. His flashlight is lying in the dirt, shining on the spot he used to be.

"Kickboxing do that too?" I say.

Tuck says, "What?"

He does a head count. Doesn't take long, even for him.

"Tuck, he ain't bullshittin'," says Billy. "There's something out here hunting us."

Tuck waves that big .357 in my face again. "Who else is out here? Your partner? Where is he?"

"Tuck, we saw he was alone. He only had the one sleeping bag."

"Maybe he's got a boyfriend. That your game, you sick freak? You and your lover come out here and get your kicks picking off hikers?"

"Tuck, that's offensive."

"I ain't saying it's bad! Not the gay part, anyway! Just the picking off hikers part!"

"He ain't gay, man. Look at his clothes. Where'd you get that shirt? Salvation Army?"

I say, "Goodwill."

"See? Ain't no gay man wearing no Goodwill shirt."

"Now *that's* offensive," says Tuck.

"How?"

"It's a stereotype. Gay man can dress however he wants, same as you or me."

"Where'd you learn that? *Dancing With the Stars*?"

"As a matter of fact—"

"Dammit, Tuck! When are you gonna open your eyes? There's a squatch out here, and it took Hurd and Randy!"

While they squabble, I try to get my night vision back. Just outside of the wobbling amoeba-shape of their dueling flashlights is a black wall, featureless, impenetrable. I stare into it, willing my pupils to dilate, to let in enough stray photons to find form in the void. Slowly, shades of gray distinguish themselves from the black.

That's when a large, shaggy shape I'd taken to be a bush starts to move.

My brain works fast. It tells me it's just the wind. Even though there *is* no wind, it's the wind. Just the wind. The wind is rustling a bush. That's all. The bush isn't standing up, reaching a height of eight feet. It's not extending a long, ragged arm, dripping with fur. It doesn't have eyes.

Green, glowing eyes.

Tuck says, "What's the matter with you? You look like you—"

My brain still insists it's the wind when the wind wraps what are clearly claws around Tuck's throat and yanks out a handkerchief-sized swatch of flesh.

It's the splash of wet warmth in my face and the taste of hot nickel in my mouth that snaps me out of it.

I wish I could say I yell a warning to Billy. But I'd be lying.

I turn and I run. Hands bound behind my back, I barrel face-first into the darkness. Branches whipping across my cheeks, feet only by some miracle not catching on exposed roots.

I run.

Behind me, Billy screams. He lets off a burst of automatic fire. It stops long before the clip is empty. So do his screams.

I don't stop. I don't look back.

I run.

I run and run and *run*.

I trip.

I face-plant into something soft. Something that smells like burnt socks.

Hurd's lying on his back in the dead leaves and brush. Eyes wide open, staring up into the canopy. I put my ear to his chest. No heartbeat. My ear comes back sticky.

I have to get this zip-tie off. Law enforcement doesn't want you to know this, but there's a little plastic tab in the clasp that unlocks it if you press down on it. You just need something slim enough to get in there. I don't have anything like that on me, so I turn my back on Hurd and start rummaging through his pockets. I find a lighter. His packet of cigarillos. A half-roll of Certs. A condom so old it could have been used to prevent the immaculate conception.

Nothing useful. I crawl over his corpse and check the other pocket.

Bingo. Set of keys on a ring with a remote starter fob. I try to pull them out, but they get caught on his pants. I yank so hard that when they come free, I fall face down in the brush.

I'm spitting out dirt and leaves when two hairy feet step into view.

Two very *big* hairy feet.

My eyes climb up two columns of brownish-black fur to the beast above. The squatch gazes down at me with glowing eyes, spaced a foot apart. Lit by their green light, its face is half-gorilla, half-wookiee. Canines the size of thumbs jut up from between black lips. It doesn't seem to have a neck, just a great shaggy head that blends into massive shoulders, from which hang two impossibly long arms that reach past its knees.

On the end dangle clumps of long, curved claws like bunches of bananas.

Up close, it stinks. It reeks of skunk and armpit, muskrat and buttcrack. A men's locker room with a dirty ferret cage in it. A septic tank filled with afterbirth.

It's the smell that makes it real. That gets me moving. I try to kick away from it, digging two furrows in the dirt with my heels. I turn over and try to get to my feet but it's futile. I face-plant again.

I close my eyes. I don't want to see what it does to me.

I feel its claws scratch down the back of my Goodwill shirt. I grit my teeth and wait for them to break skin.

It doesn't happen. Instead, I feel a claw hook under my belt at the base of my spine. It uses my belt like a handle to drag me. I play dead, thinking maybe squatches are like bears.

I don't know how long it drags me. Maybe a mile. Maybe two. I can't see a thing in the dark, and I seem to hit every single rock, root, and stump on the forest floor.

Here's the funny thing, though: Those crunching noises I heard when Tuck and the others were marching me to town? They don't stop. They keep pace with the squatch's long, loping strides.

I spit dirt out of my mouth and blow brown snot out of my nostrils. I hold tight to Hurd's keys. I wait for my chance.

Eventually, an ambient light creeps into the corner of my vision. It's a white light. Not orange. Not a campfire.

Electrical.

The squatch drags me into a clearing. No underbrush, just dirt, packed down tight. Heavy foot traffic. The squatch lets me go with my eyeballs inches from a footprint. Not a squatchprint. Not unless squatches wear boots with waffle-cut treads.

I roll onto my back. I look up into a metal grid suspended a dozen feet off the ground. Like the roof of a cage. Lights wearing metal cones hang from it. Above, bolted into the roof of the grid, are trees. But they look different.

Fake. Like artificial Christmas trees.

I roll onto my side to get a look at where the squatch brought me. It's some kind of settlement. Plywood and corrugated metal structures. Some canvas house tents. Like an army camp. Something that was supposed to be temporary but ended up being permanent enough to accrue rust and mold.

There are two Port-A-Poddies. Both bright blue, both with wooden paintings of Bigfoot hanging on the doors. The Bigfoot on the right has boobs.

Next to the Port-A-Poddies is a row of stacked cages. Like a chicken coop. Except they don't have chickens in them.

They have monkeys.

Apes, actually. Chimps. Juveniles, from the looks of it. Adults would tear those cages apart. They rattle their bars and open their toothy mouths wide to screech and hoot, as chimps are wont to do, but no sounds come out. They have scars on their throats where their vocal cords were removed.

The squatch stands in the middle of this madness. In the light, it is a sort of burnt-umber color. Its face is inexpressive. Like it's made of rubber.

A squad of hippies—both male and female, their clothes worn and faded— descend on it like a NASCAR pit crew. They disassemble the squatch where it stands. They work as a team. Efficient. Practiced. One with dreadlocks climbs onto a stepping stool and removes the head, revealing a bearded hippie face, soaked with sweat. The dreadlocked hippie reaches inside the head and pulls out a pair of night-vision goggles. He flicks a switch and their green eyes go dead.

Two others pull off the arms, revealing pink hands where the squatch's elbows were. Another hippie unzips the back, peeling the squatch suit off the shirtless hippie's torso like a NASA technician helping an astronaut out of his spacesuit.

The last step is the legs. That requires two hippies. The man in the squatch suit braces himself on their shoulders as he steps off of what are revealed to be fur-covered metal stilts, about two feet high. He's still a tall man, over six-foot, but hardly the giant he appeared to be in the woods.

Somebody hands him a bottle of water. He chugs half of it and dumps the rest over his head.

One of the hippies, a female, sees me watching. She holds up one of the arms and folds back the cuff, revealing a hand grip with four finger holes, like brass knuckles. She squeezes the grip and the claws contract into a loose fist.

She says, "Cool, huh?"

The door of a metal shack opens. Two men step out. One older, liver-spotted, bespectacled in CVS discount rack specials. He wears a filthy lab coat, formerly white, now the color of dirty dishwater. It's covered with makeshift patches and old brown bloodstains.

His companion is a stout dude, much younger. Fat all over but with muscle underneath. Stretched across his beer keg of a belly is a T-shirt with a silhouette of a sasquatch on it, plus two words: I BELIEVE.

He carries a two-foot-long metal rod that could only be a cattle prod. He closes the shed door behind him. He turns a lock and shoots a deadbolt. The door has a window in it about the size of a box of cereal. Immediately, two faces appear, peering out.

Dr. Lab Coat and Mr. Cattle Prod walk over to me. The guy in the squatch suit, now stripped down to a pair of boxer shorts, joins them. I look up at them staring down at me. Their expressions show interest but no enthusiasm. They look me over like I'm an old tree stump they're trying to figure out how to remove.

Lab Coat says, "Not much to him, is there?"

Squatch says, "I took this one because they already had him tied up. Seemed easier that way."

"The bodies?"

"Being moved. If they're found, it'll be far from here."

"I don't like it. Too much activity in too short a time span."

"Couldn't be helped. Idiots were all turned around. There were about to wander right into camp."

Lab Coat sighs. "He'll do, I suppose." He makes a note on his clipboard and motions toward the largest clapboard structure. "Send him through orientation. When that's done, tell the girls to get him ready for processing. He doesn't look too hairy but make sure they shave him for the biopsy anyway. I don't want them getting sloppy. Not now, when we're so close."

Cattle Prod lifts me to my feet like I'm made out of styrofoam. He's got the deceptive strength of an orderly, accustomed to moving bodies around against their will. He shows me the business end of his prod and gives it a little juice. Electric blue sparks between the prongs at the end.

I get the picture. I let him walk me over to the clapboard shack without complaint. We pass the monkey cage. They scream silently at me. I hold tight to Hurd's keys.

I wait.

Cattle Prod strides ahead and opens the door for me. We enter a large, dark chamber. He turns on one overhead light bulb dangling by its cord over a folding chair.

He says, "Sit."

I sit.

The room is too dark to make out much. Just shapes. Tables with stuff piled on them. Cattle Prod steps into the shadows and comes back wheeling a cart with an old cathode ray TV on it. Like you'd sign out from the AV club in the eighties. He positions it in front of me. When he turns it on, it hums. The screen glows blue.

It's got a VCR connected to it. He presses rewind on a remote control that's old enough to get a discount on its car insurance. The VCR whirs.

He presses play. The VCR clanks and clatters but no image appears.

"Goddammit," he says. "Every time, I swear to God."

He scrolls through the TV's input menu twice before landing on AUX.

The old guy in the lab coat appears onscreen, looking 20 years younger. The lab coat itself is whiter but far from pristine.

"…so you can see," he says, "why the short-sightedness of the American bio-research community has forced me to move out here to the wilderness, where my work would not be hampered by small men with no vision."

Cattle Prod says, "You good? If I have to watch this thing one more time, I'll blow my brains out. I'll be back to check on you when it's over."

He leaves the shack, letting in a shaft of light that once again kills my night vision.

Once my eyes adjust, I can tell that Dr. Lab Coat filmed the video in the same shack I'm in now. I start to make out the same lab tables and equipment I can see onscreen. The place is much more cluttered now than it was then. More wear and tear. More stuff.

Weirder stuff.

"The benefits to humanity of a functional human-ape hybrid should be obvious to all but the most blinkered and stultified minds," he continues. "But it is only here where I can perform the necessary human experimentation to complete my research. There have been…setbacks."

He stands in front of a metal rack half-filled with large glass jars. In each of them, suspended in a yellowish fluid, is a humanoid fetus. Each is irregular in its own way. Some have no eyes. Some have too many.

I peer into the darkness and spot that same rack. Its shelves are now fully stocked. Along with the jars, I can make out a plastic squirt bottle. The bottle is labeled SQUATCH MUSK.

"But the path to true knowledge has never been without obstacles. Manfully, I persevere. It should go without saying that privacy is of the utmost concern. Every day, civilization and its outmoded paradigms encroach further on my scientific haven. That is why I have taken advantage of certain local myths to scare off potential interlopers. In the early days of my seclusion, I was able to dress one of my followers—members of a ridiculous but useful Sasquatch-worshiping cult—in a store-bought ape costume, but advancements in DNA sequencing have made more elaborate methods of obfuscation necessary. Using early prototypes of my man-ape hybrid, I have been able to synthesize, via a biological printer, an easily replenished form of living tissue, complete with fur. This tissue can easily be sewn into a convincing Sasquatch costume, as you no doubt have witnessed for yourself. Combined with organic claws grown from a plant-animal hybrid, I can assure that any DNA evidence left behind will be utterly baffling to researchers."

He passes his hand over a metal table. On top of it is a large metal baking tray. It is covered with what looks like a sheet of sod, only what's growing out of it is fur, not grass. Next to it is a little potted tree, about three-feet tall, with gnarled limbs, like a rubber plant, out of which sprout squatch claws. He breaks one off and uses it to hack out a square of squatch flesh from the tray, like he's cutting himself a slice of sheet cake.

He waves the furry hunk at the camera. It wiggles like a rubbery slab of gelatin.

"Fascinating, no? The tissue deteriorates quickly, but my followers are happy to make new suits, always improving on their methods. They believe that my goal is to resurrect the extinct creature they refer to as Bigfoot, and that by imitating him in this way, they can keep his legend alive until such a time as he is able to reclaim his rightful place as king of the forest."

He sighs. "This is, of course, nonsense. But our goals are compatible, for now. With the help of an unlimited supply of a psychotropic drug of my own design, they do my bidding without question. Their primary responsibility is twofold: To scare off unwanted visitors, and to procure human subjects for testing. My process is, unfortunately, wasteful. And painful, I'm told. We try to make each subject last as long as possible but there's only so much the frail human form can withstand. That's one of the problems my research is meant to combat."

He looks directly at the camera. His eyeballs bear the guiltless gleam of the true believer.

"As you no doubt have ascertained, that is where you come in. You, sir or madam, are to play an important role in the evolution of Man, and as such you are entitled to the truth. That's why I am recording this video. I cannot promise you that your final months or years will be pleasant. But trust me when I say that your sacrifice will lead, in some small way, to a better world. Thank you, and I will see you soon."

The screen burps out static and goes blue. The hum of the TV fills the space.

By now, I've managed to work the tip of one of Hurd's keys into the zip-tie clasp. It loosens immediately, and I slip my hands out and start looking for a weapon. The best I can find is a spare pair of squatch extendo-arms, sans fur. They're just metal Terminator arms with claws, but they're heavy and sharp and I look forward to seeing how the hippies out there like being on the other end of them for a change.

I'm about to open the door a crack to get the lay of the land when I notice the unmistakable sounds of a full-scale ruckus happening outside.

First, it's declarations of confusion. Then alarm. Then the words disappear altogether, replaced by screams. Stomping feet. Howls of pain. Weeping. Cracking sounds that could be wood but isn't.

Something slams against the side of the shack, rattling the walls so hard that two jars fall off the metal rack and shatter, spilling formaldehyde and fetal man-ape across the packed dirt floor.

Then: Silence.

And then: A roar.

A defiant, rumbling, throaty, primordial roar. A lion and a bear harmonizing over a Godzilla back-up track. A werewolf with a megaphone.

It pins me to my spot. Even when blood spills through the crack under the door and soaks the soles of my sneakers.

I press my ear to the door and listen.

Nothing.

Then footsteps. Big footsteps.

Coming closer.

I hear breathing outside the door. A beast's breath, hot and violent. I smell it. Like meat and musk.

I don't move. I can't move. My pulse gallops in my ears with a double-kick beat.

I don't know how much time passes. Enough for the sun to come up and throw slices of hot light through the cracks in the walls. Enough for the birds to come out and sing an all-clear.

I drop the metal squatch arms before I open the door. I get the sense that I don't want anything on my person to connect me to these usurpers.

Something is blocking the door. I have to put my shoulder into it just to budge it.

That something is a body. Most of a body, anyway. Well, almost most. The top part, minus an arm. It's wearing a lab coat that used to be white but is now fully red.

The hippies are scattered around. None are whole. I don't look too close, but the sense is not of hacking or slashing but of ripping and tearing. Limbs litter the compound with ragged edges, like drumsticks twisted off an undercooked turkey.

The tall guy who played the squatch is folded in half backwards, his head resting on his heels. The one with the cattle prod is half in a tree.

Well, almost half, anyway.

His T-shirt has been torn from his body. It dangles from a branch like a flag of surrender. It still says I BELIEVE, but the blood makes it hard to read.

None of the others are identifiable. They're just nebulous wads of hippie meat.

The chimps regard me silently. They don't try to scream like they did at their captors.

They've witnessed the king's visit. They know he, in his wisdom, has spared me.

I open their cages and step back. They clamber out tentatively, not trusting freedom. I stay still. Avoid direct eye contact.

They scamper off into the forest. Ready to start new legends.

I check the metal shed where the human test subjects are kept. I find six of them, in various states of disrepair. They're all shaved bald, eyebrows and all. They are bandaged and bruised from biopsies and blood samples.

One of them looks fresh. His clothes are relatively clean. His face relatively unlined.

He says, "Is it still out there?"

I shake my head. If it is, there isn't much I can do about it.

"I saw it," he says.

His eyes are wide, like they forgot how to blink. The rest of his words come out in a gush.

"We all heard it, what it was doing to them. We didn't look. We didn't want to. We just hid and tried to stay quiet. But then the noises stopped. And I had to see. I don't know why. I just had to. So I crept up to the window and I looked out. And I saw it. Just on the edge of camp. Just a shape. A man, but not a man. I only saw him for a second, and then he was gone. Fast. Too fast to see him move. He was just there one second and then *poof*. Gone."

His shoulders slump. He looks at the floor.

I ask, "Are you Trevor?"

He says, "How'd you know?"

"We got some friends in common."

I lead them out of the woods, back the way Tuck and the others must have come. It's slow going. Most of them haven't walked any kind of distance in some time. Trevor and I help the stragglers as best we can.

They're very compliant. Science made them that way.

We walk until we find a trail. That trail leads to a parking area. I click the fob on Hurd's keys until a black Bronco chirps.

I give the keys to Trevor and send them on their way. I start walking in the opposite direction.

I don't go back for my gear. It's not mine anymore.

Nothing in that forest is mine.

I walk. And listen for footsteps.

Notes

Notes

Notes

<u>Solution</u>

— — 　　— — 　　— — —

— — — — — —

— — — — — — — — — — —

— — — 　　— — —

— — — — — — — —

— — — — — — —

— — — — 　　— — —

— — — — 　　— — —

— — — — — — —

A Note about Ciphers

Perseverance is not a long race; it is many short races one after the other.

-Walter Elliot

Some famous types of ciphers are known by specific names. Any cipher can be decoded through logic and problem-solving, but sometimes the best problem-solving is to work smarter, not harder. No sense re-inventing the wheel, and any other clichés you find applicable. In the meanwhile, we've provided a list that names some famous ciphers to kickstart your research about ciphers and codes, should you find yourself stuck on how to solve something you've discovered within these pages.

Affine

Atbash cipher

Bacon's cipher

Beaufort

Caeser cipher

Four-square

Morse code

Pigpen cipher

Playfair

Polybius square

Railfence

Shift cipher

Substitution cipher

Transposition

Vigenère

About the Authors

The Treachery of the Heart

Tim Jeffreys' short fiction has appeared in *Supernatural Tales*, *The Alchemy Press Book of Horrors 2 & 3*, *Nightscript 4*, *Stories We Tell After Midnight 2 & 3*, *Cosmic Horror Monthly #1*, and many other places. His ghost story novella, *Holburn*, was released by Manta Press in 2022. The sequel, *Back from the Black*, came out in 2023. Other work includes the comic horror novella, *Here Comes Mr Herribone!*, and sci-fi novella, *Voids*, co-written with Martin Greaves.

East Franklin Puzzle

R .C. Capasso has published speculative fiction in a variety of venues including *Bewildering Stories*, *Teleport Magazine*, *Spaceports and Spidersilk*, *The Last Girl's Club* and *Fiction on the Web*, as well as online and print anthologies from publishers such as *Red Cape*, *Air and Nothingness Press*, and *Pure Slush*.

Cold Food

A.M. Gray is a writer, editor, and musician. He enjoys making art in odd places—finding joy in creating new things for the world to see. He holds a BA in Music Performance with a focus in Creative Writing from Slippery Rock University of Pennsylvania. His work can be read in *Every Day Fiction*, *Rock Paper Scissor*, and *The Wordsmiths,* an anthology and novel by Hollow Oak Press.

A Lady's Work Is Never Done

Tracey Lander-Garrett is the author of the Madison Roberts urban fantasy series and has had poetry and prose published at *Connotation Press*, *Mid-America Poetry Review*, and others. After several moves from New York to Texas to Oregon, she now lives in Northwestern Pennsylvania with her husband and four cats.

The Last Case

Scott Richards is a father, writer and joke-teller from England. He is the author of *The Legend of Paper Monkey* and co-author of *The Wordsmiths*. He is also the founder and editor of Humour Me Magazine and its accompanying YouTube channel, Humour Me Comedy.

Remember That Time We Saved the World?

Kyle A. Massa is a writer living in upstate New York, and he has been previously published in *Unidentified Funny Objects 9*, *Grimdark Magazine*, and *Allegory*, among others.

Blood Road

Jessica Ritchey is an avid reader, part-time writer, and long-time lurker of the publishing world. A child of a small town steeped in history and laden with ghost stories, she's always had a great appreciation for the strange and unexplainable. She has a love for nature, including hiking and biking – though she also enjoys meandering aimlessly to take photos of shiny objects that catch her crow-like attention – and has been known to load up on caffeine and go exploring cemeteries for fun in her free time. She has an eclectic artistic repertoire and is the Associate Editor for Hollow Oak Press. Jessica resides in northwestern Pennsylvania with her partner in their house full of crazy animals and crazier children.

An Accounting of the Marchioness

Amanda Pica is a speculative fiction writer, dog-lover, and peanut butter enthusiast. She lives in a state of what-if and loves when life bends around the corners of her expectations. Her work has been published by *F(r)iction's Dually Noted*, *Story Nook*, *Wyld Flash*, and *Humour Me Magazine*. Amanda is co-author of the novel *The Wordsmiths*. She can be found on Twitter and Instagram @ASPicaWrites.

A Model Town

Mark Mitchell graduated from Cal State Long Beach with a degree in Screenwriting and currently lives in the greater Los Angeles area. His short fiction has appeared in *A Thin Slice of Anxiety* and *Black Sheep: Unique Tales of Terror and Wonder*. Follow him on Instagram @markmitchell.writer.

The Squatch

Marcel Leroux holds an MFA in fiction from Brooklyn College. The former head editor of *SMOOTH* Magazine, his fiction has been published in the *Long River Review* and *Brooklyn Review*. He lives in northern Connecticut, where he is a writing tutor at Asnuntuck Community College. *Undercover Elf*—the first novella in his series of action-comedy thrillers featuring Michael "Deak" Deacon, the protagonist of "The Squatch"—can be found on Amazon.com.

Milton Keynes UK
Ingram Content Group UK Ltd.
UKHW040230031224
451863UK00005B/351

9 798989 011827